Big Low Tide

Candy Neubert
Big Low Tide

SEREN

Seren is the book imprint of
Poetry Wales Press Ltd
57 Nolton Street, Bridgend, Wales, CF31 3AE
www.serenbooks.com
Facebook: facebook.com/SerenBooks
Twitter: @SerenBooks

ISBN 978-1-85411-583-6

Inner design and typesetting by books@lloydrobson.com

Printed by Akcent Media Ltd, Czech Republic

The publisher works with the financial assistance of
the Welsh Books Council.

part one

one

Brenda will not stir for a while. She works lunchtimes and at night behind the bar at The Navigator and afterwards she lets her mind process the voices of drunken men. As she sleeps, the latch drops at Number 7 next door and Mrs Pickery emerges, straightening her headscarf.

Mrs Pickery has a determined walk for such a little woman. She is as tough as a hawser. She is going to work in the fields, never mind that she was sixty, July gone. That is how she says it: July gone. She has her flask and a sandwich in a plastic bag and she looks straight ahead as she passes Chandra's Superette.

Mr Chandramohan sees her out of the corner of his eye. She has never bought a thing in his shop and he knows she never will. He is the infidel. On account of his name and the little red circle on the forehead of his wife and the fathomless look in his eyes.

Mrs Pickery knows for an absolute fact that Mr Chandramohan displays girlie magazines on his counter next to the till, right where old ladies have to pick up their change. She is not a prude, but what's not right is not right. She shops carefully every Saturday with her daughter and if she runs out of something midweek, it's too bad. Chandra's may be open from six until nine every day but there is nothing a body can't do without.

Mr Chandramohan lifts his eyes again as a man steps up from the pavement into his shop.

– good morning, Mr Hamon. What can we do for you this fine morning?

– twenty Bensons, mate.

Mr Chandramohan slides the packet across the glossy smile of a girl in red underwear. Franklin Hamon pulls off the wrapper and lets it spiral to the floor.

– gis a light, then.

He takes the offered matches, lights up, pulls a mouthful of smoke into his lungs and thumps his chest appreciatively.

– nice win, that Prince of Simla. Little darlin'. Had a fiver both ways.

– indeed, I remember. Your luck is changing, Mr Hamon. Your ship has come in, you might say.

– ha, ha, very funny. Chalk it up, mate.

Franklin steps out into the street again, unshaven, woollen-hatted and newly charged with tobacco. He takes the same route as Mrs Pickery, but she is already at the bus stop and seated at the front of a number eleven. Franklin crosses the square, not bothering to look out for traffic, for there is none yet, and lopes off along the harbour embankment to wait for the boat.

———

It would be fine to say that the island is volcanic, and had a dramatic beginning. The truth is that it was once a large hill, the butt end of an escarpment. Or maybe I am muddling the facts, for now I remember finding shells deep in the soil of a field and being told that the sea had once covered that very spot. Perhaps the earth heaved the island up like a blister.

It stands in the Channel, worn by the tides running this way and that over the Swinge, night and day.

We've approached from the sea like seagulls, coming in after breakfasting at sunrise with the boats. Morning Cloud and Island Beauty – they are still out there somewhere, chugging around the reefs with the light slick on their oily wakes. Who would look twice at the gulls, squawking into the air and heading for land? To be as anonymous as a seagull is a fine and rare thing to be, in island terms.

The seven o'clock flight from the mainland is also cruising in, but it has further to descend and much circling to do above the airport. We have landed first.

Here is the harbour, Port Victoria. The whole island shares its name, for the harbour is the heart and soul and the mouth. The land is fed by way of this harbour mouth, men and provender travel this way and the streets of the town digest them. The fishermen slap the flabby spoils of the sea into crates and those spoils are lifted out, packed with ice, into the market stalls. Coins rattle into the pockets of the fishmonger and tonight into the purse of his wife. Tomorrow, into the till at the grocery.

The island is an amoeba with one mouth sucking at the nutrients outside itself.

The harbour master stands in his office, glassed in on three sides as on the bridge of a ship. The water smacks the great walls down there so that at times he thinks himself at sea again, not anchored to this solid buttress at all.

We have passed the harbour master, drinking his coffee thoughtfully and gazing into space; passed the lighthouse and the old castle and the statue of Queen Victoria bearing her sceptre and crown and her heavy stone cheeks. We have passed above the market square and Chandra's and the bakery, up Turkenwell and The Steps and here we have paused. We can see straight into Flat 5, where a net curtain is blowing sideways from the open window and Brenda Duncan is lying fast asleep.

Her face is pretty but we are not seeing her at her best. Her mouth vibrates with a little snore. Her brown hair is thrown out behind her and the skin of her arm glows in the yellow light filling the room. The light centres on a goldfish bowl on the dresser; between the pots and creams there is bowl of dusty water and a fish with protruding eyes swims around and round.

two

There goes the number eleven bus, cresting the hill. It is barely seven fifteen, a time of deliveries from the bakery, an opening of garage doors and a moving of cows back to pasture after milking. A May morning full of promise, even the little cloud resting briefly on the airport.

In the parish of St Stephen's three miles away, where the land dips west again into the Atlantic, a farmhouse sits in its grey granite walls; Les Puits, home of the Duncans. Except for the Long Meadow, the surrounding acres are all leased out now to the neighbours. The driveway is tangled with weed; the garden straggles across the yard.

Peter Duncan has kissed his sons and reminded them to clean their teeth. He has wheeled his bicycle out of the potting shed and set off towards the Vine Farm. He skims round the corner and stands on the pedals to clear the rise on the other side. The bay mare from the Corbin stables barrels through a gap in the hedge, alarmed by man and bicycle as she is every morning, breaking into a skitter across the field.

Peter hasn't a thought in his head. He swings into the yard ahead of Mrs Pickery, who will hang her coat on a nail and have her overall buttoned up smack on half past seven. Jack Vine rattles towards them on a tractor, mud flaking in all directions with the turning of the wheels. Jack is in a hurry; he's a farmer. The morning is halfway over.

– morning, Mrs Pickery. Morning, Peter. Carrots to lift in number four; load the bins on the trailers, will you? Wait a minute. Clean up some of that lettuce in the cooler, Mrs Pickery, please. Chap coming at nine for six trays. Make it eight. Hitch up the trailer, Peter. We'll load up at the corner.

His last words disappear as he revs the engine into life. Mrs Pickery takes a knife from the pocket of her overall, the bone handle snug into her palm, the blade honed paper thin. She shakes a head of lettuce, slices the muddy end to the ground with the outer leaves, and tucks it into the corner of a tray. Her brown eyes shine as her fingers shake the leaves, slice and tuck. She is thinking about the first week of her annual leave, due Monday next.

———

Back at Les Puits, the kitchen is dim and cool. The clock on the wall clicks softly like a tongue in a mouth, and the cold tap over the sink drips a little slower than that. It has dripped for years and the stone sink is stained green on that side. Patrick Duncan, aged seven, stands quietly for a moment. It's a short moment but it's big. When he goes to bed tonight he'll be quiet again but the night quiet is different.

He can hear the doves up in the roof; their throats wobble. His throat won't wobble. The doves aren't fed any more but they still live there. Patrick runs his hand over his hair to smooth it down. It is curly and thick like his father's and wet enough to push flat. He wishes his hair was straight like Danny's; Danny is lucky.

He takes the cornflakes out of the bottom cupboard and the bowls and spoons and the milk from the fridge, carefully. He doesn't want his aunt to wake up but she never does at breakfast time. He hisses up the stairs for Danny to hurry, pours cereal into Danny's bowl and some into his own.

– come on.

– I'm coming.

– what's up?

– no towel.

– doesn't matter. Eat, eat.

– there's too much milk on.

Danny squirms in his chair. He is four and undersized for his age and he has a small dark face like a fox. His brother has a face which is open and freckled but his is pointy and shut. The boys wash, dress, breakfast and leave the house every day without a grown-up. Their father is lifting carrots for Jack Vine and their mother is fast asleep in Flat 5, The Steps, in town. Aunt Elsa is asleep at the end of the corridor, in the room with the funny air in it.

– give us the bowls. The milk.

– can't. I spill it.

– give it here. Get the coats.

– won't, so.

Patrick runs water into the bowls as his dad said. He takes his coat off the rack by the Aga where it hangs dry now and warm and slightly smelly. He looks for Danny's. It's behind the couch on the newspapers. The pile is as high as his knees; he checked two days ago. When it's up to his tummy button something will happen. He picks up his satchel and both coats and steps from the kitchen straight into the yard, closing the door carefully.

Danny has gone. His blue shirt is vanishing behind the last tree and Patrick has to run to grab him before he gets to the road.

– lay off.

– keep still, silly. There's cars. They'll mash you into red puddles and that'll be your blood.

– lay off me.

– stop it. Mrs Vauquier's coming and she'll see your face blubby. Where's your shoes? Oh shit.

– shit, shit, shit.

– don't say that, it's bad. Where's your shoes?

– don't know, so.

Patrick hesitates. He is gripping Danny's shoulder in

one hand and two coats in the other. He ought to find Danny's shoes; Danny will catch a chill and die, probably. But Mrs Vauquier is coming to fetch him for nursery school and he must wait with him here at the corner in case a car comes. A car is coming. A green Ford; it's her.

– hello, boys. Hop in, Daniel.

– Mrs Vauquier, he's got no shoes.

– I know. He left them in my car yesterday. Here they are. Lift your foot, Daniel. This one.

Patrick watches her take Danny's feet one by one into her lap and work the shoes into place and tie the laces. Mrs Vauquier is an angel from heaven. Mr Vauquier is the church warden and that's why. Danny doesn't know how lucky he is to go in her car; it's like having straight hair. He doesn't know he's lucky, so it's wasted.

When the green Ford starts up again, Patrick heaves on his satchel and puts his head down and runs. He's a commando running from tree to tree, dodging the bullets. Dodging his aunt's eyes which might be following him from the upstairs windows.

Long Meadow is behind the elms but she could see him through the branches so he keeps running. Over the bank he drops into the lane, safe. The bank is solid earth with grass and brambles and roots and worms and stones and she can't see through it, no one can. He has barely a mile to walk to school. It's far but its safe until after the pine trees, and then he has to look out for Melissa Corbin.

three

We've spent a long time with Patrick. His mother is asleep and she was meant to be the main character in the story, but maybe Patrick is, after all. It happens like that sometimes. Negligible things wrestle up to the surface and catch the light, and the things that seem important sink out of view.

But Brenda is stirring. She's half awake and planning things. Two ideas play in her thoughts out of long habit and each one depends upon the other.

One is getting the children back. Not that they were ever taken away but she knows Peter will be sticky about it after all this time. The little dark one is not so bad now; she rather likes him. He looks like her. After all that trouble getting him born, she ought to have him.

She needs money and a big house. That sister-in-law of hers is still living at Les Puits while she herself has this bedsit. The thought of it annoys her like an itch she can't reach. Money and a big house. She may have the solution.

Gerry Vine was in the bar last night and he could hardly keep his eyes off her.

———

Franklin Hamon has been busy for the past hour and his digestive system is much restored. The Mary-Ann is berthed in the old marina and he helped his two brothers, who have worked the south coast right round to the tower since before dawn, to load up the crates. Michael and Johnny Hamon are wet to the skin under their yellow oilskins and they stink, but Franklin stinks more. He was too busy snoring off yesterday's win to get up this morning and they have nothing to say to him. There was a good mackerel run, anyway. Should fetch a few quid.

The crates are delivered to market, the lines are loosed and the Mary-Ann puttered back to her mooring. Decks cleared and lines coiled, just so. Not a man in the harbour would leave his boat in a mess. Fishermen anyway; yachties maybe.

Franklin is rowing them back to the quay in the dinghy. He wants to row; it clears his head. Johnny has a wicker pot on his knee.

– got lobster, eh?

– yup.

– big 'un?

– yup.

– sellin' 'im?

– nope. Givin' 'im for the draw.

– ah, yes.

Michael holds a rung of the ladder while they climb out. Johnny slips the pot back into the sea under the dinghy and secures it with a rope. The lower rungs of the ladder are rusted and barnacled and water slops up behind them, shifting the green weed. At the end of the slipway the two of them shuck off their oilskins while Franklin slips a bowline through a ring. Then they head for the Yellow Box.

Leaning against the walls at the top of the wharf, the café is a construction of wood and corrugated iron entirely painted yellow. Painted some while ago now, and peeled and faded, but nonetheless box-shaped and yellow. In the inner sanctum Mac the Knife stands in the ten-foot square from which he creates vast breakfasts for men of the sea and the occasional landlubber curious or lost.

On this side of the hatch, large men sit at small tables. Every head is covered, flat caps or woollen. Gnarled hands grapple with knives and forks, beards are wiped, smoke exhaled companionably across the plates. Johnny Hamon pulls an extra chair forward and thumps Franklin on the back.

– your shout, you lazy sod. Mine's a special with two eggs.

– an' mine. An' chips.

– greedy bastards. Okay. ''Ere, Mac! Three specials

double eggs one chips and three teas, strong.'

– my tea ever weak? Eh?

– keep yer 'air on. Sorry, mate – I forgot.

Mac turns his bald head back to the fryer and grins. Franklin weaves back to the table, taking a circular route.

– awroight, mon vieux?

– awroight. Et tu bion?

– weh.

The Hamons sit back, light cigarettes, crossing their feet under the table, one over the other.

– seein' that Louise tonight, you?

– might.

– oh-*ho*.

– might not.

– mn.

– know that lobster?

– mm.

– old Hen'll be right chuffed, him.

– ah. Worth a bit.

– he'll only give a fuckin' ploughman's for it, tho'.

– ploughman's hell. 'S worth four pints.

– Brenda'll get 'em.

– ah.

– know what?

– eh?

– Brenda don't like 'em. Scairt of 'em.

– so?

– so what say we give her a surprise. Little present.

– nice one. Yeh, tea's 'ere. Push up. Chips, thank Christ. I'm starved.

———

Up in Flat 5 the light has brightened and strengthened and lost its granular appearance. Brenda is stubbing out a cigarette as she gets out of bed. She pulls a dress off the rail and holds it against her nightie and then throws it down. She leans across the dressing table and peers into the mirror and pulls the skin at the edge of her eyes outwards, baring her teeth. She smiles a wide smile and then a little one. She narrows her eyes which are narrow anyway, and this gives her a knowing, feline expression. She sits and thinks into some place in the future.

There's a tramp on the steps and a knock on the door.

– who is it?

– us, Brend. Open up.

– this ain't the bar, you know. Morning, boys. I'm not dressed for company.

– yeh you are.

– shut the door then – him next door's listening; he always is. I'm getting back into bed and sitting like this – and you can sit there. Mind my foot, you big booby. What you holding your coat like that for, John Hamon – what you got in there?

– somefin' for you, darlin' … 'ere … 'an 'ere … TA DAA!

– oh! Get it off!

In the bathroom at Number 7, Wilf Pickery holds

himself in mid-flow. He juts his head towards the adjoining wall, concentrating.

The lobster has hunched back on itself. Its blue plating settles noiselessly, dry and crisp and knobbled and mysterious on a landscape of nylon and wool. Its eyes look, and register God knows what. The antennae swivel painstakingly through the air.

– ugh! God in heaven. You dirty pigs! I hate you! Get it off the bed now, now, NOW.

The three men are laughing too much to move. The lobster, finding itself free, lifts a claw and digs it into the blanket, edging forward. Brenda scrambles onto the dresser, pulling down her nightie and tossing things to the floor.

– oh Lor, the goldfish. Look what you've done! Listen, you scummy lot – I'll never serve you again, never.

– yer will! Henry'll make yer. It's his bar.

– I'll get you banned.

– oh yeah? We're 'is best customers. 'Specially when we give him this little beauty for the draw.

Johnny plucks it up and takes it through the open door to the tiny kitchen.

– never saw yer move so fast, Brend.

– look at this mess! Bleedin' heck. Flippin' bowl's cracked; me fish'll die.

– stick 'im in the teapot.

– better empty it, eh!

– yeah, imagine that swimmin' round yer cup.

– goldfish an' three sugars please.

– yeah.

– I've had enough. Get on with you, go on – out, out! Shoo!

– aw'right, darlin'. Still love yer. See yer t'night.

Wilf Pickery stoops on the inside of his front door, lifting the letterbox with one stained fingernail. He hears the men blowing noisy kisses and sees a flash of Brenda before she slams the door. A second scream has him riveted to the spot. Brenda has found the forgotten lobster in the sink. The old man looks down at his trousers and rubs at a wet patch. Ah well, they'll dry. It's sunny out.

four

The streets of the town are veinous and narrow. For each one that is level there are three that snake up the hill, sloped and stepped and channelled in the middle by centuries of feet. Victoria is an old port. King John's men looked across the walls and loosed their arrows at Cromwell. It is an old port. The houses swarm over the hill and the hill folds back for its covering of cement and brick and stone, but this will change it as little as barnacles change the rock to which they cling. The shells shuffle and fall away, but the breath of the rock is not at the surface and the sleep of the rock is very deep.

———

Brenda clips across La Soeur Street in her little heels. She swings along, a woman just thirty, full of life and well-being and shopping for underwear. Gerry Vine is on the up and up. She smiles to herself. He's been in London doing something or other – business, anyway – and he's just moved into that enormous house at Le Clef. It isn't possible to make a move undetected on the island – that must be why he doesn't see her often in public, while their affair is getting established. These little white silky things won't do it any harm.

A little later, she is sitting with Jackie from the shoe shop in a window seat of the Grange Bar.

– 'ave one of them pies with me.

– I couldn't. I'm not hungry.

– it's love, does that. I can't stop meself. Go on, stop me, Brend.

– just eat it, silly. See what I bought.

– oh gor. Look at them little flowers. What d'it cost?

– never mind. Guess what those Hamons did to me this morning.

– they never.

– put a lobster in my bed.

– they never. Dead one?

– no. It's walking about in my bath.

– it never.

– know that Gerry Vine?

– 'course. Skinny and sunglasses. Thinks a lot of himself. Heard 'e come into money. That pie was delish. I feel awful; I blown me diet. You should've stopped me.

– you seen him with anyone?

– you in love with Gerry Vine?

– no. Just wondering.

– there's that Susan Pickery look – out there. Won't see

him with 'er, anyway. She's a right priss.

Susan turns at the corner at the end of Turkenwell and greets Mr Chandramohan in his shop. She knows that her mother is running out of sugar; today is Susan's afternoon off from the old peoples' home where she lives and works, and she can discreetly replenish supplies. She doesn't understand the fuss about the magazines; they're only pictures, they don't hurt. Her mother is set in her opinions and that was the trouble with people, that's what happens to them.

———

Mrs Pickery has stopped for lunch. Jack and Peter have gone and she sits on an upturned crate in the shed, just in the doorway with the sun on her knees. She unscrews the lid of her flask and sips the sweet and watery tea. She chews a sandwich slowly: jam. A yellow newspaper lies under the corner of the bench, a calendar two years old hangs on a nail, the bagging machine for potatoes stands to one side. The chute needs cleaning. Dust motes speckle the air. Mrs Pickery is thinking; will she let her Susan in on the plan, or not? Bit more complicated if not, but more satisfying.

———

Danny Duncan rides on the bicycle with his father, home from nursery school. He sits with his legs over the handlebars and his hair flies straight back off his head and his eyes water in the wind. Rockets hurtle through space, dolphins burst out of the ocean, a great black horse thunders across yellow grass like the one in the painting at Auntie Deborah's. The last bit is best – fooosh! Past the church and the white wall and the gateposts and bump bump bump down the drive without slowing down.

The best part of the day is followed by the worst. Sitting in the kitchen for lunch with Dad and Aunt Elsa, then Dad gets up to do something else and Aunt Elsa talks to him, Danny. She has a great mane of hair and red lips. She is also very thin and wears strange clothes with silver belts. She laughs with sudden shrieking noises and nubs the end of his nose with her hard fingers; once the cigarette fell out from between them and stung his arm like a nettle.

Peter Duncan has his third cup of tea and goes back to work. For Danny there are two hours alone at Le Puits with his aunt before his brother comes home, and in this time he usually succeeds in avoiding her entirely.

Sometimes he goes to the hen house where the hens purr softly in their boxes full of straw and he won't come out even when Patrick is home and calling for him. In the winter there are indoor places like the back room, behind the curtains – not hiding places, for there is no one to hide from. Elsa is busy sorting out papers and turning out cupboards and moving furniture.

They are just places. Outside in the Long Meadow there are any number of these places. Danny can flatten himself between two tussocks of grass and disappear like a hare in a form. And then there are the wells.

The wells are at the bottom of the land in the field behind the hen house, forbidden ground. There are two wells and the first is sealed, but a pebble pushed under the cover with a thin stick will sometimes make a tiny plip! into the inner waters. The second has a pump poised above it. Wooden planks have been jammed into place making a crude lid, rotten now with the damp of long winters. Danny can look into the blackness and see the mirror sheen below. The wells are the place for bad days and Sundays. Today it is the hole in the hedge.

five

We are having difficulty meeting Elsa Duncan. We've tried to call her out but she hasn't come; she is like that. We can know that she is thirty-nine and arresting to look at and fills us with unease, but not much more.

Patrick is also asking himself questions about his aunt; they are second only to the great unspeakable question in his heart. At two-thirty Melissa is waiting for him at the school gate.

— your aunt's a witch, Patrick Dunkhead.

— leave off.

— she shot her husband.

— who says?

— everyone. She's a mad witch. She's been in the mad house. There.

— leave off, pig.

— and you're a bustard.

— I am not.

— Dunkhead's a bustard! Cowardy cowardy custard!

He runs, he must always run, but round the corner he slows down; she won't follow. It's possible that his aunt is a witch. It would explain his mother leaving. Maybe Aunt Elsa was jealous when his mother had babies. Maybe she cursed his mother, and stopped her liking the babies. Maybe the second baby – Danny – belonged to Aunt Elsa really and it was his mother who was jealous? Was the dead husband somebody's father? Maybe he lay in the churchyard over the wall at Le Puits. He'll stop and have a look; there's no homework.

Instead of crossing the Long Meadow, Patrick takes the longer route by the lane. The lychgate is open. He walks slowly around the stone slabs of the cemetery, as familiar to him as his own backyard. He knows the little group in the corner where the name Duncan appears many times. Henry Duncan son of… Vera Duncan beloved wife and mother. There are no clues. Perhaps people who get shot are not put in the same place as everyone else. It seems as though all the names might mean something, but they never do. He likes it here.

He turns to go and gives a sudden cry. It's only Danny's face between the bars of the gate, looking. He does that – he's just there, looking. Quiet. He's on another planet if you let him. Patrick brings him back to normal quickly.

– hi. Bet you can't climb up.

– what you doing?

– gonna race you back. Give you a start, count of five. One, two, three…

———

The smell of beer hangs heavy but not unpleasant on the air. The Navigator bar is a dim brown hole sparsely decorated with a spotty mirror and a framed display of fisherman's knots. Willy le Cras sits at the corner of the bar with a pint of mild. He looks fixedly at a row of pint glasses hanging from their hooks above the bar, each one belonging to its own regular customer and emblazoned with a crest of their favourite football team.

Brenda is noisily filling up the shelves beneath the counter from the crates which Henry, the landlord, left in the doorway. Guinness, milk stout, lager, ginger, lemonade, Coke; all stacked up to the edge with no gaps. The shelves will be emptied by eleven o'clock, and running up and down to the cellar and back is something she doesn't need. It's bad enough when the beers need changing. Or the gas bottles, even worse. Henry's primed the pumps; the barrels should last the night but you can never tell. The darts league will be here by eight and that lot from the King's Arms might turn up, and there's the draw. Thank heavens Henry came over to remove the lobster from her bath; now it's in the icebox, good and dead.

She kicks the empty crates away and then rubs at a mark on her black high heels with a licked finger. These heels are plain stupid behind the bar, but the lads expect it. They probably hope she'll slip. Not the old ones, like Willy there.

– all right, Willy?

– oh aye.

– will I top her up, before the rush?

– aye.

The door swings open, admitting two men. Brenda reaches for their glasses and fills them before she is bidden, two pints of bitter top.

– looking smart tonight, boys.

– 's Friday. 'S the league, innit. Give yer a game, Bob. Gis the chalk, Brend.

By ten o'clock The Navigator is full. Willy le Cras has slipped out, making his way in the warm haze through the lamp-lit streets. His corner seat is too near the scoreboard; he doesn't feel safe when there's a darts match, it's not the same.

Men are crowded against each other now, standing sideways to the bar with one arm holding their drinks firmly in place. In the far corner a man from The King's Arms is taking on the opposition at the pool table. Sid Corbin has laid down his cue in disgust. Franklin, Michael and Johnny elbow their way through from the match.

– we're mashing 'em. It's a whitewash.

– fill 'em up, Henry.

– this ain't a garage, mate.

– aw, get on with it. 'Ere, Brend! A man could die of thirst in this place.

– you wait your turn, Micky. I'm serving this gentleman here.

– servin', eh? Do your 'ol man know about it? I'll give you a service anytime. We boatmen are good at it.

– cheek. My ol' man's got a boat, thanking you.

– yeah but it ain't got no engine, gorgeous. My engine's a great big beauty. Smooth runner 'n' all.

– your mouth's a smooth runner. Three pints coming up.

– on the house, ain't that right, Henry?

– you're joking. The last two rounds were on the house; I'm counting.

– hangy me! Fer a luvverly lobster like that?

– it ain't gold-plated, is it?

– go on, then. Have one yerself an' all.

Henry clangs a ship's bell for attention.

– all right. Time for the draw.

– lobster, innit, eh?

– yeah. Whopper, 'e sez.

– FAUGH!

– What's up with Johnny?

– EYUK! Thez a fuckin' fish in me beer!

– nah! Let's 'av a look...

– bloody 'ell he's right y'know!

– look at that!

– that's nivver beer. Tha's water.

– that's a bleedin' goldfish.

– ha – that's a good un. A bleedin' goldfish!

– Brenda Duncan, I wants a word wiv you.

– oh yes?

– put this poor little bugger in a bucket. I reckon you 'n' me should sort this out outside.

– an' I reckon we're quits. If you think I'm stepping outside with you, you want your head examined, John Hamon.

———

She kicks off her shoes, and her stockings soak up the wet from the floor. She dumps the ashtrays into the sink and swills them out in the black water. That Gerry. That no-good big-mouthed lying sod. See you later, he said. That meant later, today. Got six minutes to go, then. She wouldn't have worn this silly bra if she'd known he wasn't coming.

– go on, love. We're all shipshape here.

– thanks, Hen. I'm whacked. Someone's chucked up in the loo.

– I'll deal with it. 'Night, love.

– night, Hen.

six

The familiar black car draws up as Brenda crosses Main Street. He leans across to open the passenger door, and she slides in meekly.

– where're we going?

– Italy.

– what?

– it'll taste like Italy. Look on the back seat.

– oh, Gerry! I'm too tired.

– too tired for me?

– no; to drink wine at this hour.

He doesn't answer. The car is part of him, his long legs tucked comfortably into its body, his hand resting on the gear stick. Obediently it soars away from the town, turning corners, closing gaps, thrumming into the darkness after the thread of its own headlights. I'll be his car, she thinks. She raises a hand unconsciously to the lace trim at her breast. The island is eaten away under their wheels.

On the gatepost, the name of his house, mellowed into

stone; Le Clef du Ferme. The solid proportions of the walls blur into the night garden, dipping into the leaves of camellias for an instant as the car swings to the front porch. He peers forward, leaning on the steering wheel as a hawk might sit on a dead rabbit. The hunch of shoulder, the fold of wing, the slow moment before the jabbing of the beak. He flicks the car back into life.

   – aren't we going in?

   – no.

   – are you taking me home?

   – you want to go home?

   – no.

   – I'm just driving.

―――――

In the bedroom at Les Puits, Patrick lies awake. The wind has strengthened and the elms bow and curtsey to its song, touching the hen house roof. Bows. Boughs. Perhaps that's why boughs are called boughs. The bowing boughs. The boy tries to shuffle back into sleep but his ears are alerted to sounds. There's that funny hooshing noise in the wells; his dad says it's the same as blowing across the neck of a bottle. He's tried it.

   It's a northerly wind, blowing the trees like that. If it's gone round to the west by Sunday they won't take the boat out. Low tide at two. Tide's probably on the turn now; that's why the wind's suddenly come up.

   He hears the back door close, the movements of

someone in the kitchen, and then his aunt's tread in the corridor towards her own room. She is a nocturnal creature. They've just done that at school. Owls and bats and hamsters; they are nocturnal creatures.

———

On Sunday the wind has dropped. Still blowing enough to fill a sail; just right. Patrick has hurried out of church and waits anxiously while his father talks with Mr Vauquier. They're discussing the hedgerows; the lanes haven't been cut in the neighbouring parish; it is early summer and the weeds will seed. Unfairly these seeds will blow across the fields of St Stephen's. Plus the ragwort is bad for grazing. John Corbin's hedgecutter could be hired; Peter will have a word with him – he's a cousin on his mother's side, after all. Jack Vine will loan a tractor; it's all family, since his Deborah wed John.

Patrick shifts from foot to foot impatiently. They must change out of their Sunday clothes and make sandwiches and take Danny to Auntie Deb's before they can even begin.

Behind the group of people murmuring in the church porch, Danny is jumping on and off the stones which edge the path. Mrs Jessop catches sight of him.

– Daniel Duncan! Dear little boy. Come and let me kiss you!

Danny takes one look at her bearing down on him, her large bosom quivering under a wild paisley print, and he is off over the tombstones and the wall and across the fields.

Patrick tugs at his father's elbow in dismay. Danny could be gone half the day and they have to clear the reef two hours either side of low water.

– right you are, Mr Vauquier. I'll see to it in the morning. Won't forget. Bye now.

– Dad! Danny's run off – bet I know where. The hay barn at Mr Corbin's.

– mm. What time's low tide?

– 3.47.

– right. We can leave by... twelve thirty, easy. I'll fetch the lad and take him straight to Deborah while you go home and change. Are you old enough to pack up the lunch?

– what'll we have?

– surprise me. I'll do the flask. Off you go.

———

The oars are smaller at the ends but even so they are too big for his hands. It's difficult to row without splashing but he can keep straight now and not spin about in circles as he used to. The outgoing tide helps, and his father has given no word of instruction. Patrick is the captain.

The Nan is swinging gently on her moorings in deep water. She's an old lifeboat from a big ship, her curved planks overlapping. Clinker-built, Dad says, but Patrick prefers to say, overlapping; it sounds more watery.

He manoeuvres the dinghy alongside, remembering to lift one oar early to allow for drift. They stow their things aboard – picnic, water, coats, oars. Peter knots the painter over a cleat and lets the dinghy slip astern. He's the captain now.

The boat noses away with the light airs fanning her sail in little puffs. On this side of the reef the orange buoys mark the lobster pots, a string of plastic baubles over their death traps, trailing long chains down into the dark. Patrick stares after them. This might be a good time to ask. It might. But unless a question comes out straight away it grows bigger in his mouth and it won't come out. His father cradles the tiller as if he likes silence.

They cross the Piqûre Rocks swiftly. The boy watches the Nan's shadow running alongside, slipping into the gullies and leaping up towards him where it is shallow. Seaweed and stone, green and brown, silver and gold. The ocean on the other side is another water altogether, the air across it colder; it goes all the way to America. He keeps his head down; the boom is swinging about.

They're headed for the lagoon where the reef curves. The flat pool appears only on very low tides – two boats are here already in the lee of the rocks and they wave towards these as they pass, dropping anchor at a good distance. Peter busies himself with the sail, which, folded, reminds Patrick of a kind of pastry.

– why've you got blue eyes, Dad?

– mm?

– I mean, and not me. Or Danny.

– it's genetics.

– will I get genetics?

– ah. It's not something you get. Well, you do, I suppose, but only in the beginning. Then it's just the way you are.

– is Aunt Elsa a witch?

His father hesitates for a moment, and then gives a slow smile.

– I might've thought so once or twice, years ago. What put that idea in your head?

– they say she's mad.

– who does?

– at school.

– ah well. They say a lot of things, some right and some not. Your aunt is more an... unquiet soul.

– oh.

There's no sound for a moment, and the boat sings the cadence of the sea.

– is Mummy an unquiet soul?

– no. Come on, let's open up this bag, then. See what we're having for our Sunday dinner! Two packets of crackers – good for seasickness. Cheese, apples, good. Knife, good chap. Beans? Is there a can opener? Never mind. The marshmallows look interesting; let's start with those.

They eat, and their words sift away further and further from their hearts. Later they take the dinghy into the reefs, taking turns with the oars. The tide percolates out through the pools and swirls back again. The surfaces turn from green to white to red and the earth pulls round and the sun stays behind to shine on America.

———

They cycle home in the twilight. It isn't far, but it's up-hill, and Patrick has the exhaustion of the sea on him. In the kitchen he drinks milk and smiles at his father and feels the salt prickle on his skin under his clothes.

Upstairs Danny sits up in bed, and watches him with bright eyes.

– I been playing with Melissa.

– yeah?

– yeah.

seven

In Number 7, The Steps, Mrs Pickery is busying herself in the kitchen on Monday morning, making her flask for work. She made the sandwiches last night, and while the tea draws in the pot she puts the sauce and pickle on the table for her husband. Her overalls were washed at the weekend as usual and are now folded and clean for work, which poses a bit of a problem. For Mrs Pickery is not going to work.

She takes a cup of tea upstairs to the room once occupied by her daughter and now by her husband. She leaves it on the bedside table and he opens one watery eye and grunts.

Downstairs she fills her flask with milk and sugar and tea and rinses the teapot. She riddles the fire and banks it up with coal, making the same amount of noise as usual; it's years since she was quiet for him, ever since he took early retirement, really. She gives a little snort. Anyway he says he's getting deaf so he can hardly complain about noise, can he?

In the hall mirror she ties a headscarf under her chin and then appears at the front door, letting the latch fall behind her. She turns left and heads down Turkenwell towards the square, then turns sharp left again, and then again. Up the passage where the bins are kept, behind the estate houses to her own back door, for which she has a key at the ready. Very quietly she closes this behind her, creeping light-footed with her bag to her room. Then she slips back into bed.

Wilf Pickery sleeps on. At about ten o'clock he sticks his feet out from beneath the covers, and then his knees. He sits for a moment and scratches at his vest. Slowly he pulls on his trousers, goes to the bathroom, coughs, hawks, flushes the toilet.

In the kitchen he sets the kettle on the hob and pokes the fire, making it collapse. Mrs Pickery nods in recognition of every sound. In the pause she knows that he's lighting a cigarette and reviewing the racing results in yesterday's paper. He will make himself a ham and pickle sandwich. He'll flick cigarette ash into the coal scuttle, a habit she abhors and which surely puts him on the level of a pig. In about forty minutes he will leave the house and make his way to the Swan, where he'll arrive a few seconds after opening time.

When he's gone, Mrs Pickery sits up and pours herself a cup of tea from her flask. For a moment she listens attentively. Wilf says you can't believe the goings on next door sometimes, and she doesn't want to miss anything.

However, from Number 5 there is penetrating silence. She turns on the radio and settles back into the pillows.

———

The silence next door is due to emptiness. Brenda has at last woken up in Le Clef du Ferme, to where her desires have led. She sits now, mid-morning, at the bedroom window, squinting pensively out into the garden. There is the lawn where she and Gerry were locked together last night; last week it was in a field — she's read about this kind of thing. An outdoor lover. It adds a different angle; it's not a problem, though rather chilly.

There's something at the back of her mind she can't quite recall from the heat of the moment — the phone had sounded in the house, but that isn't what she remembers; it had only given a few rings. No, there had been another sound... a door shutting maybe? Perhaps it is usual to feel overlooked, lovemaking out of doors. Perhaps that is the whole point of it.

This morning there's no sign of anyone having been here, hardly even of Gerry himself. His clothes lie on the chairs, his wine glass lies on the floor, he lies in the bed. But Brenda has been to the kitchen to make tea, and found no tea to make. No tea, no coffee, no milk, no edible anything. Only clean white tea cups hanging in the cupboard, and a bone dry kettle.

All right, Mr Weirdo, she thinks; I'll find my own breakfast. She slips her dress, crumpled and rather muddy, over her head, and crams her shoes and stockings into her handbag. She gives the sleeping Gerry a long look, but he does not stir.

The rooms of the house spread out from the corridors. It seems a hotel without the staff; Brenda can almost fancy she sees a chambermaid slipping behind the door. She gives her head a little shake to clear the nonsense away. On the driveway, on the road, her bare feet feel the cool surface as they haven't done for years. They will become sore, but she doesn't mind. She has forgotten her uncertainties; she is concentrated elsewhere.

In the Cross Keys Café she orders coffee and toast and seems unaware that the manager and his wife stare at her from the kitchen. Brenda has never believed in love at first sight. On the island where everyone knows everyone she has always known Gerry Vine. She is a le Cras and so is his grandmother; they are of a kind.

Full of breakfast and a dazzling new energy she walks home, swinging her bag and her hair and saying good morning to cows standing at hedges. Jack Vine, in a field, sees her pass and lifts his cap and rubs the back of his hand across his eyes, shaking his head. It was his father who married a le Cras, the second time. They always were a bad lot, in his opinion.

eight

The questions form of themselves as we move from here to there. Dipping in and out of place and time we must wonder about Brenda, aware that some crossing of molecule and atom sent her away from her children. She herself never queried the terror that came to her when the dark head of the second-born snuffled against her chest; it was too vast a fear to probe. She never wanted Peter to touch her again.

She may not try to understand it but her sons will pick up the thread and unravel it or not as they will.

The one with the freckled face thinks about her and the one with the pointed face looks out at the world with her eyes.

———

In the hallway of Les Puits, home of the Duncans, the phone rings.

– hello?

– who's that? Patrick?

– yes?

– it's Mummy. Hello?

– hello? Yes?

– I thought we could go out to tea somewhere; there's a place called the Cross Keys where they keep parrots. I'll pick you up from school tomorrow. Shall we? Hello?

– and Danny?

– mm? Yes, of course, and Danny. All of us. Tell your dad to bring him along. All right?

———

Mrs Pickery is having the time of her life. Every day this week she has hugged to herself the special joy of hearing others go about their business. She never knew before the fine view of Mr Chandramohan's backyard to be had from her bedroom window while pressed up against the wardrobe. She has seen that one next door return home at odd times and wearing peculiar clothing. Wilf returns at ten past three every day, after which he falls fast asleep in his chair. Mrs Pickery is then able to retrace her route of the morning, risking the neighbours' eyes, returning through her own front door at the usual time.

She once considered plunging her hands into the flower beds and rubbing earth into her overalls, but some delicacy prevented this.

By the end of the week she's completely rested. There was no argument about where to spend the holiday, no difficult task of coping with Wilf away from the public bar at the Swan, and it hasn't cost her a single penny.

———

The island is an amoeba with one mouth. Amoeba-like it changes shape with the currents through the millennia and people can feel the currents and the changes in their lives, if they stop to listen.

In the north-east runs the Swinge where the tides running up the Atlantic coasts of Europe prepare for that narrow sphincter between England and France. The waters squeeze and jostle, producing surface ripples on a dead-calm day. Here the helmsman feels the rudder taken from his hand and the keel play games out of keeping with the wind and knows, for a moment, fear. If he has a motor he'll wonder at its changing heartbeat, and the faltering bite of the propeller.

In the south-west there is a mirror image of the Swinge where vessels wallow and drift. Here is the bay where the Nan swings on her mooring, and the reef we've already crossed with Patrick and his father. A little further lie the rocks and the waters called the Avaleur, the swallower.

As the Port Victoria lighthouse swings its night-time arms in the east, so the Avaleur lighthouse sweeps the south-west coast. Flash, flash, and pause. Flash, flash, flash, and pause. Boats still ride up on the rocks, even the great tankers, when the crew are sleeping and the green eyes of the radar scanners bleep unnoticed on the bridge.

Some fishermen know the east coast and some the west, but every heart pulls with the tide and hears, on some level, the waves that break out there in the dark.

nine

They are lifting potatoes in the south field, Jack and Peter
pulling brown gashes in the earth behind the tractor,
separating one canvas sack after another from the pile,
shaking out the dust of last year's earth. Stacking a new
pile of filled sacks on the trailer, dust in their eyes, in their
beards.

   — right then. That's a good lot. Fetch the forks, would
you, Peter? Behind the seat. Aye. We'll go round the
verges.

   — she could rain, I reckon.

   — she may. But we've time enough.

Peter Duncan would wish this a day on the sea and not
on the land. He questioned Patrick closely about what
she said, and knows that the boy answered faithfully. An
invitation to tea. Today. The Cross Keys. All of us. He has
not counted how long it is since they saw her. Months.
He and she have withdrawn into their territories like
wounded animals. He bled for this woman and just

managed to staunch the flow. Now – tea; all of us.

––––––

– who you waiting for ?
– someone.
– I asked a question, Dunkhead. Who?
– my mother. She's fetching me.
– poo! Your mum's got a man.
– she's not.
– she has too. She does it with him on the cliffs. Your aunt that's a witch told my mum.
– leave off me.
– don'cha believe me? Danny does.
– go away, Melissa.
– I'm going anyway, Spot-face.

Patrick scowls. He waits by the school gates as the cars pass and he stands forward hopefully and then he stands back half out of sight, searching for that face. Then a black car stops and his mother leans out of the window and her face is bright and smiling as she waves, and beside her is a man.

––––––

In the Cross Keys Café, Peter stands at the counter with his youngest son. It was good of Jack to let him off early but still, he feels awkward.

– if you take a seat, sir, we'll take your order at the table.
– ah, we're waiting for someone.

– Dad, I want some of that.

– what's that, Dan?

– that one. That chocolate one.

– maybe. We're waiting for your mother.

– and Patrick?

– and Patrick.

– I want it now.

– well, we're going to wait.

– *now!*

– listen, Dan, listen. We have to wait and then we'll choose together. Come on, let's sit here. Look – look out there; all those parrots. And gnomes. Take your fingers out of the sugar. What's the matter?

– I want cake.

– soon. Here, wipe your face. That's it.

He hears her voice before he sees her and then he sees her and is not prepared for it. The soft wraps desert him and the bleeding starts again. He rises to his feet and at the same time sees a man whose face he recognises but doesn't associate with this moment, until the worried eyes of his first son look from the man to himself and establish the connection.

– oh Peter, it's you. Hello.

She seems surprised to see him. He pushes a chair back and touches Danny's shoulder: you asked me to bring him. She lifts her sunglasses over her hair; speaks again.

– well, shall we sit, then? Hello, Danny. Have you seen the birds? Peter – do you and Gerry know each other?

She seems surprised to see him.

– I'm not staying. I just brought the boy. Have to get back now.

– oh stay, for God's sake, and have some tea or something.

– Dad!

It's Patrick, pulling his sleeve. He nods his head, or shakes it; he doesn't know what he is doing. The man, Gerry Vine, sits down, stretches out his legs, and takes out a packet of cigarettes. Peter steps across him; outside, he lifts his bicycle and cycles away through the weightless air.

———

The time is out of joint. He knows that is Shakespeare but where does it come from? The time is out of joint. He ought to be working now and he turns towards the fields where he left Jack, but then he remembers the clean clothes on his limbs and that his work clothes are at Les Puits. Jack will be taking the tractor back to the sheds before long and Peter would prefer not to look him in the eye just now.

He turns away from the road he travels every day and there are neat gardens and hedges and greenhouses he barely knows. A new light falls strangely for him even as it has for her, which she can call love and for him it is the other pain. The lanes leading to the cliffs are laced in white, hawthorn and allium. Peter throws down his bicycle at the end of the path and walks to the edge.

He drops down through the gorse, pulling off his clothes, sending the scree flying. At the foot of the cliff the gulls rise up squawking and circle over his head and a cormorant lifts its wings, keeping close to the water. The tide is heavy and full and slides lazily on the rock. He doesn't know this place and resists the thought of diving. He lowers himself into the bitter cold sea and feels the surge of it, thank God, thank God.

At home he arrives feeling oddly purged. He expects all to be as usual but the boys are not yet home and only his sister sits scribbling at the kitchen table. He fills the kettle and sets cups and spoons on a tray; normality is a thing which he must hold in place with both hands.

The black car turns into the drive just after six. His wife climbs out and follows the boys to the porch and kisses them while the man stands by the open door of his car looking the house up and down, and into the front hall. Elsa watches him through the window and smiles. Then his wife and the man return to the car and close their doors and go away.

– Dad?

– I'm in here.

– he's got a great car, Dad it's got an extra seat in the back and I sat on it. And I did the lights. And the horn. Arrr! Arrr! And I had chocolate cake twice. And ice cream.

– Patrick? You all right?

– yes, Dad.

– don't suppose you'll be hungry now?

– no.

– and you didn't say goodbye and Mummy says you're rude!

– that's enough, Dan. Patrick, d'you have homework?

– no.

– so you two feed the hens and collect the eggs. I'm going to evensong; I'll be back by bathtime.

Peter hasn't been to vespers for a long time. It's a short service and there are two hymns and he will stand next to Bob Vauquier and he will sing.

———

Driving away from Les Puits Brenda lights a cigarette for herself and one for Gerry and considers the last couple of hours. Successful, on the whole, she thinks, even Peter's sudden departure, which just shows him up for what he is. And look how Gerry spoiled the kids.

– nice clock he's got there.

– clock?

– in the hall. Le Noury. Good piece. I'll have that. Like to get a better look.

– the grandfather clock in the hall? He'll never sell that. You're joking!

– been in the family long?

– friend of his grandad made it, or something.

– thought so. Nice piece. I'll have it; you'll see.

– you're very sure of yourself.
– that's right.
– where're we going?
– just down here.
– you'll have to take me home – I'll be late for work.
– you won't be late. Don't you trust me?

ten

Elsa Duncan still hasn't said a word to us. It is tempting to slip into her thoughts, but that's a dangerous exercise. It is eleven o'clock at night when she folds up her papers and returns them to the chest in the morning room which is now called the back room. She slides her pens into the flat drawer of the escritoire. Upstairs there is no sound; her nephews and her brother are asleep.

He is dreaming of a stampede of horses over a flat plain and three of them have riders. One of them is his woman and he wants to run to a knoll in the distance for safety but his feet will not move, and he tries to call her but his voice will not call.

By the back door Elsa puts on boots and a coat and steps out into the yard. She listens to the night for a moment as a fisherman might listen to the dawn. The moon is up but hidden by cloud. She sets off at a good pace through Long Meadow and down the empty lanes.

At the entrance to the Corbin's farm the dog lifts its

head. Recognising her step he runs up the bank to meet her and trots beside her a little way, pushing his head up into her hand before turning back to his post.

On the corner by old Bash's house she pauses, hearing a sound. She melts into the hedge as the door scratches open. The old man moves across the step, a wavering light behind him picking up the hairs on his head. He stands and pees into the long grass, then sniffs and sighs and moves back inside, closing the door.

In the lanes bordered by trees there are thick lakes of darkness but she can see her way, even so. In the fields above the south coast the land lies open and blue under the stars and every field has a gap in the hedge which she knows. She skirts the ploughed land and crosses the fallow as the cows shake their tether ropes and the rabbits show their white scuts.

———

It is hundreds of years since the pillars of the old harbour were sunk into the mud. Slimed and thick they carry the warehouses and customs office and the Yellow Box, all still and shuttered now in the night. Through them seep the tides. The stones of the new breakwater shelter the hulls of yachts in the marina and one day they'll vibrate to the engines of passenger ferries bringing a thousand tourists from the towns of France. But not yet. Through the stones and the pillars seep the tides and the green ghosts of fish.

Half a dozen fishermen have cast their lines into the dark beyond the lighthouse. The cars come and go on the Victoria Pier. In a station wagon piled with ropes and lobster pots, Johnny, Franklin and Brenda are wedged into the front seats, eating chips.

– what d'yer reckon our Michael's up to, then?

– Louise, ain't he.

– she'll get 'im down the aisle, I reckon.

– yeah. 'E took 'er drivin' Sunday, round the island all la-di-da, and we'd 'ad that conger in the back all day Sat'dy and Christ did it pong.

– think he's showed 'er his lunchbox then do yer?

– ah yes. Why not?

– never thought he 'ad it in 'im.

– 'ad it in 'er, more like.

– ugh, Franklin, you're so crude, I can't stand it. Leave my chips, you; you've had your own.

– I've got such an appetite, my luv, me 'ands move by themselves. Least you're smilin' again. 'Ad such a long face at the bar I though' yer chin 'ad got caught in the till.

– well, I'm off home now. Ta for the chips.

– 'ere, we'll take yer 'ome.

– no fear… you'll have all the neighbours hanging out of their windows, I know you. It's only five minutes. See ya, boys.

At the corner of Main Street the light is on in the telephone box. Brenda opens the door and props it open with her foot, diluting the smell of urine and cigarettes with the outside scent of the harbour. She dials the number of Le Clef du Ferme. It rings and the receiver is lifted at the other end.

– hello? Gerry?

The receiver is replaced and the telephone shrills a continual dull note into her ear. As it did last night. She looks at her watch. Ten to midnight. She kicks the door. Perhaps Gerry called at the flat while she was out. Well, she was out, wasn't she.

———

On Saturday morning Susan Pickery drives the Morningside Retirement Village minibus along the narrow road which joins the top of The Steps, where her mother is waiting.

In the back sit five elderly ladies and Mr Farthing, the most able and sprightly residents of Morningside. Every Saturday the minibus is used for their outing and Mrs Pickery has managed to overcome her reluctance to travel in their company. It's not that they aren't nice people; very nice. It's just that she, Hilda Pickery, is a working woman, and much younger. However, having a lift home with the groceries is much better than the bus, saving some money, and there's always the chance of information to be gleaned from the dusty old brains sitting in the back.

For instance, that one with the thin, pinkish curls, Mrs Aileen Vine, née le Cras. Mrs Pickery already knows her to be the stepmother of her employer, Jack, and mother of Jack's half-brother, Lucas. Now this Lucas has a son called Gerald, who'd be in his thirties. Mrs Pickery has reason to believe that the man with the long black hair who comes next door to visit the estranged wife of her colleague, Peter, is one and the same person – Gerald. She dwells upon this extraordinary connection, voicing the fact that if they should ever marry then Jack and Peter would be related, and for the second time, so to speak.

– shhh, Mum. Mr Duncan's not even divorced, and listen to you.

– young folks divorce at the drop of a hat these days. Sooner he's shot of her the better. You should hear her next door sometimes. That one Gerald isn't the only one, you know.

– yes, Mum. Let me concentrate a minute. Traffic's terrible and I've got to park near the door.

In the supermarket there is a difficult moment as Mrs Avery tries to negotiate the turnstile with her walking frame. Mr Farthing wants to be chivalrous and gets in the way until Susan separates the entangled chrome, sending Mrs Avery one way and Mr Farthing another, and losing sight of her mother.

Mrs Pickery has sped off on her usual route anti-clock-wise, beginning at the cereals and finishing at the toilet paper. There is a reason for this. The dairy section flanks the household goods and if the butter comes last then it has less time to melt before she gets it home. At the open fridge she spies Aileen Vine by the frozen peas.

– look at these petit poys then, eh.

– terrible price, see that. You keeping well, Mrs Vine?

– they looks just like peas.

– and your Lucas, mm?

– ah, he's a good boy, that one.

– and his Gerald, doing all right?

– you not buying any then?

– they give me wind. And you?

– ooh no. They feeds us at the Home.

– everyone's all right, then?

– oh they do us lovely. Custard's what I like.

On the way home Mrs Pickery considers that Gerald Vine can't have come into any money through his family, and therefore probably did so by less than honest means. Which proved again the kind of company her next door was in the habit of keeping. Didn't Susan agree, Peter was well out of it?

– poor man, with those boys and all. I'll look after them more often for him. Tell him, Mum.

– oh yes and we know where that'll lead, my girl. You don't fool me. And him not divorced yet and all.

eleven

It's hard to say now, with time tucking up into itself as it does, whether a week has gone by or a day. It is the same for them, for the man in the field, the man on the road and the man fishing at the harbour with half a bottle of rum resting against a bollard. And for the one in the armchair and in the cradle and in the pub it is the same. A change will come and the difference between happy and sad is whole age and one or the other may last for years and be no time at all.

For Brenda a coat of blankness has been lifted from her shoulders. She lives in hours and days of love and anxiety. If she expects to see her lover that night he will not appear for a week, and if she doesn't expect him for a week he'll be there in ten minutes. She has never been so alive – though she doesn't always like it, and won't let it go until she gets it right.

For Peter a contentment has slipped and revealed the seed of sorrow underneath. Just as she took his seed and threw it out and left him with the nourishing of it. Now the vague belief that it will all work out for the best is shaken into pieces he cannot gather up.

———

On Sunday after church the boys stand about awkwardly and say no to every suggestion and then quietly announce that they are going out with their mother. Through a smile which pains him, Peter notes that the man, Gerry, is not mentioned and the shadow of him is cast deeper and longer because of this. Then he wonders when the arrangement was made, and the chill of unmentioned things creeps into the house and into the telephone, a miasma drifting through all the safe corners.

———

He rows out to the Nan with no purpose in mind and spends the afternoon feeling the breath of the new god, jealousy. He strips off his shirt in the June sun and empties the lazarette of its fenders and ropes, finding a scraper and a stiff brush and stepping again into the dinghy. Beginning at the stern he cleans the belly of the boat at her waterline, holding her gunwales with stiff fingers and eyes half closed in the glare. Back in the cockpit he sits for a while with his hand on the tiller and looks over the stern with a measuring eye and taps the planking with his feet.

He would like to still be sitting at sunset but instead

he rows back to the shore and leaves the dinghy upended above the tideline. He cycles home with sunburned shoulders and a more peaceful heart. As he turns down the lane he's surprised to hear a droning noise he can't identify and a little less surprised to see the black car like a cockroach at the door. The illusion of a great insect increases with the droning sound as he leaves the bicycle in the shed and approaches the house. The teapot stands on the kitchen table, warm to the back of his hand. Through the open window he sees Brenda, Elsa, Patrick and Danny standing in the Long Meadow, all looking up at a model aeroplane which putters through the air with a tiny engine guided by Gerry Vine.

Peter is drawn to the window and he too, watches the machine spinning on a thin wire. First he will march out and order his wife to leave with the man and the car, and then he imagines her laugh and perhaps the laughter of his sister. Then he imagines the eyes of the children and he checks himself. Next it seems that he himself should be the one to leave and cycle away and throw himself into a pit. Then he balls his hands into his pockets, takes a breath, and walks outside.

The other man is absorbed in the flight of the plane, which dives and coughs and finally plummets nose first into the grass. The boys cheer and rush over to carry it back as he stands coiling in the wire. Brenda joins them and they stand in a cluster as Peter approaches and hears them speak.

– that was a flippin' great one ! It must've gone round a hundred times.

– wheee! Wheee!

– what's the damage – let's have a look. Only the propeller, we can straighten that out; it's not broken.

– what about this – is this part of it?

– looks like part of a fuselage.

– ... it's got a fuselage...

– get me an elastic band.

– anyone got an elastic band? Oh. Hi, Dad.

– hi, Patrick.

– your nose is all red. Look at his nose.

– hi, Dan. Hello.

– he's got a great plane, Dad, and it's for us; it runs on real plane fuel, you should see it go!

– I saw. Yes, I saw it. I'm just going to... make a sandwich. Can I... sandwich anyone?

– we've been eating ALL day. We had marshmallows in the car. We ate 'til we were SICK!

Peter turns to the kitchen again and Elsa turns with him and he is grateful. His woman and the man skirt the house as Danny rushes past and rummages in the kitchen drawer for something. By the black car the man and Danny fiddle with the plane while Brenda speaks to Patrick and then she slips into the car with a graceful movement and they are gone.

―――――

Seven days a week from six until nine, including Christmas, Chandra's is open. To the islander, the ways of the east are strange. There was an ominous murmuring from the shopkeepers of Port Victoria when Mr Chandramohan first threw open his shutters, nearly twelve years ago. Yet the goods move fast on the shelves and have no time for gathering dust. Never mind that the prices are a little high; Chandra's is always open.

It's open on Sunday and Gerry stops here for cigarettes. In the car he throws a magazine onto Brenda's lap and she looks in surprise at the fleshy expanse of the cover girl.

– what am I supposed to do with this?

– anything you like.

– I don't want it.

– chuck it out then.

– you're a screwball.

– that's me. You're learning. You can make me a cup of tea.

In Flat 5 Gerry gets into Brenda's bed with all his clothes on while she busies herself in the kitchen. She throws the magazine into the bin and cups her own small breasts for a moment in her hands. The road of love seems a little more circuitous than she'd expected, but then, she thinks, it's like that, isn't it? One person's straight is another person's crooked. She sugars his tea and carries it to the bed, noticing how thin and scrappy he looks, waiting for her, like a little boy.

twelve

Peter unpegs the dry clothes from the washing line. He folds them into the wash-basket and silently blesses Susan Pickery as he carries them indoors. She comes once a week to do the ironing – just the boy's shirts really; his own work clothes don't need it, if he hangs them out carefully. He irons his own for Sunday; it only seems right. This week Susan offered to cook a meal before she left, but he wouldn't hear of it.

– Patrick! Patrick!

He listens in the doorway. The house is quiet, and the yard. The hens peck disinterestedly in the dust.

– Patrick!

– coming... yes, Dad?

– fetch Danny, will you, and we'll do the hen-house. Change the straw.

– Danny's off.

– where now?

– I don't know. I looked, earlier.

– never mind, we'll do it. Will you help me?

– sure.

– Okay. Let's fill the buckets.

The water gushes noisily into the tin pails.

– coming out on the boat this weekend? Tide's good.

– yes, I guess so.

– anything wrong?

– no.

– you worried about something, eh?

– no.

– worried about Danny going to school next year?

– I guess so. A bit, maybe.

– he'll be okay.

– yes.

– he'll come out of himself; make friends.

– Dad?

– mm?

– mum wants us to live with her. She said. She said not yet but soon.

– ah well. Well. She is your mother. But I can't see that happening. No. It just can't be. There's not room for the two of you with her. And it's too far from school. Maybe she'll come back here one day; that's what she means.

———

It's hard for men and women to receive signals from each other, even when those are clearly transmitted in words and behaviour and an infinite number of means besides.

Brenda doesn't hear what Gerry is saying to her; she has her own agenda.

Peter likewise believes in his own assurances until the truth wriggles through and presents itself to him at the wheel of the tractor three days later. Brenda won't return to Les Puits, of course. Gerry Vine, of whom he has refused to think, has recently come into money, hasn't he? Think! He's bought a big house, hasn't he? Rumours of poker games, huge stakes, huge losses, huge wins. Think, think, think about it, go on; pull it open, eviscerate it.

In the seedling house on the farm he brings in the washed trays ready for the next planting. Mrs Pickery fills them with compost and flattens it with a piece of wood and drops a seed into each square with practised fingers. Jack carries them down the house to lay them out on trestles under sheets of cardboard. At the end of the day they lift the covers and turn on the sprinklers so that under a fine mist of water the seeds awaken, and when Mrs Pickery replaces the covers the little skins will split in the moist soil, tomorrow or the next day, and the kernels will begin to grow.

Mrs Pickery doesn't see that Peter has returned with another pile of trays and set them down behind the crates. He hears her talking to Jack and at one time would have minded his own business. Now it is his business, and he hears.

– how's your Simon settling back?

– ah he's doing all right. Misses the bright lights.

– friendly with your step-nephew, is he?

– Gerry? They're of an age. He's a bad lot, that one.

– is it?

– through and through.

– I heard that our Peter's Brenda, that lives next to me, is seeing something of him.

– Simon?

– no, Gerald. And she's no better than she ought to be, neither.

– poor man.

– Gerald?

– no, our Peter.

Later, when the protective skin is split and the kernel growing, Peter asks Jack if his son, Simon, can remember how to drive a tractor. Jack replies yes, he supposes so, and then wonders at the question.

———

On Saturday morning Mrs Avery, Mr Farthing, Mrs Vine and their friends are enjoying the countryside. The mini-bus fairly hurls along the leafy summer lanes, not towards the town but towards St Stephen's, and they haven't been this way for... oh, ever so long. They are going to the shops later, yes, but Susan is looking after two boys this morning, and picking them up by the church. What's that? Too much noise? No, it's lovely and quiet here; must be your hearing aid crackling. Susan says we're taking the scenic route, isn't she a one. Lovely petunias there, see!

Isn't that a new wall? I don't remember it being there.

At Les Puits Patrick and Danny are delivered into the bus and they sit freshly scrubbed and subdued amongst the powdery smiles. Susan tells Peter that she'll make sure they have lunch before she brings them home, not to worry, and under her words she wishes him ease and she wishes him love. Peter pumps up the tyres of the bicycle and sets off for Port Victoria.

At the harbour the fishing fleet is in and the decks washed hours before. The dinghies drift on their ropes by the pier like a corps de ballet. Peter looks down at them, noting particularly those with outboard engines, and then he wheels the bicycle over to the Yellow Box and props it against the wall.

Inside there is a brief but not unfriendly lull as he enters. He nods towards one or two familiar faces and goes to the hatch to order tea and a cheese roll. He sets this down on the table where the Hamon brothers sit, and sinks his teeth into the food.

– 'lo. Peter Duncan, in't it?

– 's right. Mm. Hungry. Cycled across the island. I'll have another.

– Mac! Gi's another roll fer this lad 'ere. Doing all right then?

– right enough.

– you got a little clinker, in't it?

– 's right. Not so little. Twenty-six footer.

– ah. Pretty, she is. Used to 'ave a moorin' this side.

Seemed a little tiddler over 'ere. I remembers 'er.

– I'm looking for an engine.

– is it?

– maybe. Think so. Want to fit her out a bit.

– ah. Engine, eh? 'Ere, Mac! Seen 'Arry this morning?

– eh?

– seen 'Arry? 'Arry from the Cloud?

– ah yeah. Bin an' gone.

 -Ah. 'Arry's got an old Enfield, ain't 'e? Eh, Franklin?

– yeah. Big fucker. Air-cooled. Usin' it, tho.

– is it?

– runs 'is generator, don't it, fer the vinery.

– ah.

– 'member that Kelvin we started with? Petrol and paraffin job. Fweh! Make yer jump overboard, one of 'em. What you want? Twin-cylinder, is it?

– 'e's better off with a single. Long-stroke with a big fly. Nice slow revvin'. Hand start it easy, then. What you reckon?

– sounds good, aye. Know of any?

– there's that Mahy chap. Bill Mahy. 'Ad a Lister, eighteen horse. Wonder if 'e sold it already?

– 'e won't come back today. Football's on. Arsenal's at 'ome.

– nor tomorra. Church.

– tha's right. But we'll ask fer yer.

72

thirteen

On Sunday the wind blows. Danny has gone to the Corbin farm after church, where John Corbin and his wife Deborah are harvesting soft fruit in the kitchen garden. Melissa and Danny disappear into the orchard – the blonde head and the dark just visible above the grass.

The Nan flies along, free as a bird, free as a fish. The island diminishes behind them; slowly the Avaleur slides across the horizon and the Marais Tower looks like a box on the cliffs, a hat, a blur. Reluctantly Peter changes course for the long tack home. Now he is the one nursing the question, choosing his time.

– Patrick. Y'know what you said the other day? About living with your mother.

– I don't want to.

– I know. I thought not.

– can she make us?

– she's said nothing to me as yet.

– but she will?

– seems likely, aye.

– can she make us, though?

– depends.

– it's up to you, isn't it?

– not if the law says otherwise. Anyway, I thought we might go away for a while. On the boat.

– oh yeah! France?

– no, no. I've cousins in Ireland; place called Cork. They were sent over as children in the war and settled there.

– you mean we'll sail all the way?

– well, boat needs a bit of work. Maybe fit in an engine in case of emergencies.

– emergencies?

– ah, just in case. Winds and currents act funny round the Scillies, I'm told.

– sillies?

– at the end of England.

– coo! What'll we eat?

– we'll get plenty of provisions on board. Like the sound of that?

– Danny too?

– of course. Can't separate brothers.

– but Dad, there's school.

– when's your holiday?

– five weeks time.

– there you are, then. Five weekends to get her ready. Evenings too.

– great!

– Okay. Keep it to yourself for a while. Time to loose off a bit now. Mind your head.

———

Such a rational man, bearing the coils of fear like any other. Fear of edges and falling and loss of love. It is not like Peter, this plan, yet the thoughts connected to it enter his head with their clever accomplices. There are schools in Ireland – so that problem is sorted out. Elsa can sell Les Puits if they don't come back, for what is a family home without family, without sons? They'll live for a while on the capital. They can come back one day; it need not be forever. Just until the ache is gone. When the boys are bigger they will be different from the little ones he has held and cleaned and knelt beside at night. But not yet.

Every long midsummer evening, Peter rows out to the boat. Her keel is good; she was out of the water and anti-fouled last winter. She is snug and tight and trim. He fixes the masthead light, new hanks for the sail, and a little stove in the cabin. He stores tins and dried milk and sugar in the lockers and matches in a plastic tub. He buys charts of the south coast of England and clips them up against the deck-heads. He is almost happy.

Once he comes home when it is nearly dark to find the minibus in the yard and Susan standing at the kitchen sink. She turns with an apologetic smile and he says wait, I must say goodnight to the boys first, and he is upstairs a long time, sorting out their clean clothes for the morning. Downstairs she finishes the washing-up and wonders if she should leave, and then she begins to clean the stove. Peter comes down and sits at the table and watches her.

– I finished the ironing and young Patrick came to me with a tin of beans and said he couldn't work the opener. I made a pie – only took a minute. It's still in the oven, if you'd like some.

– well... I could do it justice, I'm sure. But Susan...

– I know. It's not my place. But I was free this evening...

– Susan...

– It was no trouble. I'll just finish this and be on my way.

He watches her. Over her hips she wears an apron which he remembers; it must have been in the drawer. The strings are tied around her where she is strong and round and wholesome and the unbearable sadness comes back. His hands could no more reach out for Susan than his vocal cords speak Chinese. He filled the wrong woman with children and that's when the pain began.

– that's finished, then. I'll get my coat.

– here, let me. Susan, thanks for all you've done.

– it's nothing. See you next week, then.

– yes, next week.

– goodnight.

– 'night.

———

In the bedroom at Le Clef du Ferme, Brenda is lying awake. She is thinking inconsequential things, of the shampoo she brought to Gerry's big white bathroom and then she ended up washing her hair back in her own flat. She hasn't managed to get a grip on the situation; she always ends up where she started.

She thinks of the phone calls. When she's not with Gerry, she calls him, and always he lifts the phone and then will not answer her. Yet tonight the phone rang and he drew away from her and spoke into it for a long time, and she had an image of her own self in the telephone box and of Gerry, finally talking to her. She feels split into a lesser version of Brenda; she must push out, become real and whole, get a grip.

She turns over and curls her legs against his and slides her hands around him.

– Gerry? Gerry? Love me?

– whrrr? mmmf.

fourteen

Patrick tips water into the little metal bowls. The big red's laying has gone right off again; there are only two eggs today. He wishes that Danny wouldn't stand in the doorway; they're supposed to do the hens together but Danny just stands there, blocking the light.

    – you going out on the boat with Dad again on Sunday?

    – yeah. 'Spect so.

    – and me?

    – no.

    – don't care. You don't know who I saw at Melissa's.

    – who?

    – won't tell you.

    – doesn't matter.

    – I saw mummy's boyfriend.

    – so?

    – he gave me chocolate. And I drove his car. So I don't care.

– don't care about what?

– you and Dad.

– me and Dad nothing.

– you are. You go off together.

– you're coming with us.

– where?

– away.

– where away?

– Ireland.

– what for?

– I'll tell you. Mummy might try to take us from Dad so you and me and him are going on the boat. It'll be great.

– no! Won't!

– sh. Don't tell. Don't say nothing.

They stare at each other for a moment over the scratching of the hens. Then Danny turns away and disappears. Patrick places the two eggs carefully into the front of his shirt, holding it up like a little hammock. He picks up the watering can and crosses the yard, his feet heavy with the weight of his heart. He pushes at the weight to keep it hidden. Now he's betrayed the plan – did his father actually say it was a secret? No, but betrayal is a big monster and he can't look it in the eye. His father just said: brothers can't be separated. He can't look that in the eye either.

———

Danny skirts the fields on the inside of the hedge, through the land now leased to the Corbins as far as the grass bank bordering the road. Perhaps it's not so odd for Patrick to wonder if his brother is Aunt Elsa's son after all. The two of them are both skirters of fields and walkers of borders. Does it really matter to the nature of the child, which is the seed and which the carrying belly?

We too are watchers, following him now, this mean little dark man-child of four, nearly five. He works his way towards a wooden construction on the hedge, a simple three-sided box that serves as a market stall. On the one side, facing the road, Aunt Deborah's strawberries are for sale. There's a rusty cash box with a slit in the top for coins. Unfortunately for Danny the box has a small padlock now, since Deborah found that the money did not match the sales of fruit.

He crouches in the blackthorn where he is hidden from the house. He is very still and very patient. There are no voices and no cars approaching, but he remains still and patient for that is what he is good at, and he is sunk deep into himself. Now he moves to the side of the stall where the strawberries shine scarlet and squeaky fresh in the shade. He plucks one from each tray, twelve in all, drops back into the field and sets off in a curious scuttling run.

By the pump straddling the big well he tucks himself between the struts and lays his prizes on the wood. The green pips knobble the soft red skins down to each pale white base. He pulls off the calyx and eats them one by one.

———

Thursday night is Brenda's night off from the bar. Henry knows that a man's drinking habits are directly linked to his wage packet and so on a Thursday he can manage The Navigator on his own.

Brenda is at home, in the bath. She smoothes her legs and rubs oil into them, twiddling the taps with her toes. There's no hurry; Gerry is never early. They roam the island at night on a Thursday – a game of pool at the Kings, or maybe another mad fool scheme with his step-cousin, Simon. Dead boring place, Port Victoria, really, but Gerry makes it different. He gives off an electric current, you get sucked in, you sizzle in it. Brenda is sizzling now as she wraps a towel around herself and pads into the bedroom. Gerry likes black. Black skirt? Black stockings?

When she is ready she lights a cigarette and sits at the window. She hears the clattering of pans from the next door kitchen and sees Mrs Thingy from the bakery put their cat out. They'll be going to sleep now, her and her husband, and get up at three in the morning to mix another load of dough. Brenda and Gerry will just be having it off in a field round about then – funny what keeps people busy at different times, she thinks, flicking the cigarette end out of the window. She got Wilf

Pickery right on his cap once, but it didn't catch fire and he never noticed.

There's hardly a ghost of day left; the late evening sky seems to be boiling coal. Through a gap in the rooftops Brenda sees the lights of the harbour and the tiny red and green eyes of an approaching yacht. She pages through a magazine and tosses it down. Then she turns off the lights, picks up her bag and locks the door behind her. She'll wait for him at the top of the steps.

There are headlights but quite a different car continues down the road. Maybe Gerry will park at the bottom of the steps? You can never be sure where he will be. She clatters down and gazes along Turkenwell. She walks to the corner and watches the traffic on Main Street and the lights from Chandra's spilling over the pavement. There's nothing she needs to buy. Better to go home, and not seem to be waiting for him at all. Maybe he has even arrived while she has been out, and found her door locked. He wouldn't hang about.

Back in the flat she feeds the goldfish. Then she lies back on the bed and stares at the ceiling.

At quarter past eleven she sits up again. The single striking of the town clock has broken her reverie and something snaps inside her. Right. Very well. If you don't come to me, I'll come to you.

fifteen

Normally Brenda would change her clothes before walking across the island at night. Normally she would not walk across the island at night, but she doesn't feel normal. A finger pushes at the back of her neck, pushing a button; she is propelled along. Her stockings chafe a little at her thighs and the northerly wind blows on the back of her head.

If she remembers walking these roads in the opposite direction, sunny and in love, it doesn't slow her now. She takes a slightly different route, crossing the main roads and keeping to the back lanes, and only a few cars pass. Caught in their headlights she walks with purpose and assurance. Left in the darkness she is a feral thing, tracking her mate.

There are two cars outside Le Clef du Ferme. She takes off her shoes and walks around the lawns, close to the hydrangeas and avoiding the squares of light which fall from the upstairs windows across the grass. Her eyes feel big and white and treacherous.

There are voices and a sudden burst of laughter. She climbs the black sheet of the garden wall, driven up easily by the pushing finger. She stares into the bedroom, into the face of her sister-in-law. Elsa is not looking back through the glass; she is playing cards with Gerry and Simon, who sit on either side of her on the bed. Simon speaks, nods, raises a glass to his lips. Elsa throws a card down, lifts her arms over her head, throwing off her shirt in the same movement. Bare-breasted she smoothes her hair, and seems now to look straight out of the window. Brenda ducks. Her feet falter on the wall; she crouches, scrabbling for a grip. She slithers down, tearing something. The choice is there to ring the doorbell and to burst open the box. She takes a step or two – but that will spoil a dream too good to lose. She'll think of something else.

Out in the lane she remembers her shoes. She pushes back through the hydrangeas and feels about in the flower beds. Guilty as a thief she breaks out of the shrubs and runs away.

It is almost one o'clock. The beer drinkers and the darts players have all gone home long ago. One car passes on the main road and in a distant lane Brenda flattens herself into a bush. If Peter had a car he would pick her up and take her home. Or if he should just walk by, he would pick her up and take her home.

———

The doves trill on the roof. Patrick sets the table for breakfast, two bowls, two spoons, and the milk. Then he opens the second drawer under the cutlery and takes up the brown envelope that holds his father's pay packet from last week. Often he has seen him slide the drawer, consult his envelopes and return them to their place. It is good money, the safe, solid money of potatoes and carrots ready to be exchanged for cornflakes and oranges and things from other soils. There are three crisp ten pound notes left. Patrick removes one and folds it into his pocket and closes the drawer. The tap drips into the sink; the doves trill on the roof.

– Danny!

– what?

– come on, it's ha'past.

– coming.

All day at school, the folded note is in his pocket. It has a voice of its own which only Patrick can hear. In the lunch break he locks himself in the toilet and unfolds the note, quietens it and slips it away again. Through the afternoon lessons it sits in the cloth at his hip, humming its soft little chant.

After class he is away at a run, too quick even for Melissa. No one is waiting at home, anxious if he should be late, but he has never been to shop in St Stephen's on an errand of his own before, and the thing is itching to be done.

―――――

On still summer evenings the west coast paints an image of beauty and happiness. The Duncans walk from Les Puits down to the coast, Elsa too – drawn to the flat ink sea and the crusts of rock and the soft sun lowering down. Elsa sits on the slipway and Danny wades into the pools with a bucket while his father and brother row out to the boat. The Nan rests in water so shallow that they can see the crabs walk the sand beneath.

– seems we're almost done. Let's get a second coat of varnish on the tiller. This weekend I should find out about that engine – then we'll start loading up with supplies, eh?

– I've got something for you, Dad.

– ah! I wondered what you had in that bag of yours. Hey! Chocolates? What's...

– they're your favourites.

– they are. They are, right enough.

– so you won't just have beans and stuff.

– just a minute – how long have you been saving your pocket money?

– I found it.

– found it?

– the money. In the hedge. On the way to school.

– just lying there in the hedge?

– yes.

– ah. Okay. Tomorrow morning we'll have a walk along and you show me just where.

– aren't you pleased, Dad?

– with the chocolates? Of course. Thanks, mate.

– don't ruffle my hair! Your hand's all varnishy.

– but we'd better take them back, all the same.

– back?

– to the shop.

– what for?

– it wasn't your money. Someone's missing it, maybe.

– oh.

– we'll see.

– there's all flies stuck in the varnish.

– poor little devils. We'll sand them off when it's dry.

Later, when the grains of sand they have brought from the beach have settled into the carpet, Peter goes up to the room where the boys are asleep. Danny is curled with his face to the wall, Patrick on his back with one arm flung outward. For a while the father stands over each child. Then he goes back to the kitchen and opens the second drawer.

sixteen

– what's the matter, love?

– I'm okay.

– quarrel with your boyfriend?

– honest, Hen, I'm fine. Just a bit tired.

– a bit tired! Jeez, Brend, you've got bags under your eyes I could fetch the shopping in.

– aw, shut up!

– Keep yer pecker up, eh? I can't spare you tonight, or I'd send you home.

– that better?

– awful! Here're your mates. They'll cheer you up.

– 'evenin', 'Enry. Evenin', Brend. Cor blimey, look at yer! You 'ad a barney with yer fancy man, you?

– don't you start, Franklin.

– I don' mean nothing, you know me. Aaah, th's better. Nivver insult a lady that pulls a good pint.

– you never remembers to pay for it, neither.

– it's our Michael's shout, tha's why. Oi, Mickey, me

lad! Git yer 'and in yer pocket. You 'eard the news, Brend? She's got 'im!

– who?

– gettin' wed, ain't they? Ain't that right? October, prob'ly. First 'Amon to go under!

– don't listen to 'im; 'e's wild wiv jealousy. Ta, Brend. 'Ave one yerself.

– congratulations, Michael. When you bringing her in?

– tomorra, if these two behave themselves.

– course we won't. Let the poor lass see yer in yer true colours, eh, Johnny? What do you say?

– I say it's the end of a great pool team. The 'Amons from 'Ell will never be the same.

– don't be daft. I'll still be playin' Fridays.

– tha's what you say, that's what you say! No, sirree... You'll be too busy fixin' things...

– an' mowin' the lawn...

– at night?

– yeah, at night! An' feedin' the baby...

– what baby?

– what baby, he says! You got a lot to learn, Michael! Lo, Bill. What you 'avin'?

– pint top if yer don' mind, Franklin. Congratulations in order I hear, Michael. Mac the Knife tol' me. Good lass, is your Louise. Ta, Brenda. I came to see you boys about that Lister.

– ah yeh. It were Brenda's ol' man that were askin'.

– I hear you, talking about me.

– nah, yer ol' man. Want's to buy Bill's engine.

– only maybe, like.

– he on the phone, love?

– what's he want an engine for?

– 'is pushbike, yer reckon?

– very funny. Didn't he say?

– doing up 'is boat, ain't 'e. Going off somewhere mebbe.

– Brend! Need some service down 'ere!

– right you are.

———

He didn't come into the bar; he wasn't even waiting for her outside. There is almost relief with the disappointment – Brenda needs to be fresh for him, sparkling fresh and at her best. Now she is drained and hollowed out where she has wanted him, now, for more than a fortnight.

She sits on the edge of her bed, peels off her clothes and hunches her shoulders. At this moment she might cut out of her life this no good thing – instead she wants the very opposite. Had she ever told him how she feels? Has she proved herself sincere, committed to him no matter what? No. So he too must be full of uncertainties. Perhaps he can't see it clearly until she, Brenda, reveals it to him.

The eyes of her sister-in-law have stared back at her since last night. Even those sudden breasts stare with their nipple eyes and connect with her own and her own dark ache.

Soon after two in the morning there's a knock on the door which she does not hear. She's sleeping a restoring sleep, clear of dreams, but Mrs Pickery hears it and sits up in her bed. She ghosts into the next room and wakens her husband.

– Wilf! Listen! Wake up! Wilf !

– eh? You what?

– shh! Listen!

He blinks for a moment at her nightie and a happy memory almost asserts itself but not quite. Then he too hears the knock.

– it's 'im, come for 'er. What a time to be a-prowling! Sixteen past two it is. I can't quite see...

– come away from the window, woman!

There is an urgency in Wilf Pickery's voice. The magazine he found in the next door's rubbish last week is tucked behind the curtain.

– there he is! I see him plain as day. Oh Lord – hark at that!

Brenda wakes up now to the rain of gravel chippings on her window. She is dredged up from the thick of unconsciousness, running half awake to the door. He is here, of course. Of course he is here. Sleepily she falls back into bed, wrapping herself around him. This is having and holding, for better or for worse. He hasn't taken off his shirt, silly boy.

seventeen

In the morning the boats have unloaded and half the catch is already sold from the market place before Brenda and Gerry stir. Mrs Pickery has passed Number 5 with her eyes straining, and now sits in the minibus on her way to the Co-op, annoyed that the news of last night's late visit is a morsel not big enough to be worth telling.

Brenda opens her eyes first and knows that they look puffy. She consults the mirror; yes, they are. She rearranges the pillows to support herself in a sitting position to help the puffiness subside, moving carefully, not to disturb him. She kisses his shoulder. She is as clear as a scoured-out bell. When he turns and slides a hand across her, she offers him anything in the whole wide world.

– two sugars.

– oh, you!

She will do it, then. He comes to her for tea; he shall have tea. When he is fully awake but with the pockets of his mind still empty from the night, she will sense her moment and slip into it.

– Gerry?

– mnrr.

– you know the kids?

– mnrr.

– school holidays next week.

– and?

– and I thought we could ask them to stay for a while at your place. They'd love the garden.

– you getting all mumsy, are you?

– no. I just thought it might be fun.

– sure. I'm easy. Where's my tea?

———

Patrick is walking with his father along the back lanes. He never walks this way on a Saturday; everything looks the same, although it feels quite different. His father talks about nothing in particular, but the silence between his words is as loaded as a gun.

Peter senses the drag in his son's feet and wonders if he is doing the right thing. He doesn't know how to bring this out into the open; he has not met deceit in the child before. He trusts him. He has the box of chocolates in a bag under his arm.

– so where did you find the money – round here somewhere?

– there. About there, I think.

– sure?

– not really... I... not really.

Peter sits on a low wall and pulls the boy towards him gently.

– Patrick. We're past the turning to school and you said you found it on the way to school. What's going on? Mm?

– I just... I don't know... I'm sorry.

– hush. It's all right. It's all right. This going away bothering you, is that it?

– we're not. We're not coming.

– not?

– it's Danny. He wants... he doesn't want... oh...

– don't cry. Here. Poor lad. What's Danny been saying?

– says he wants to live with *him*. You know.

– does he now. And you?

– you said brothers can't be separated.

– I did? I guess that's so. What do you think? Patrick?

– I don't know.

– come on. We're sitting on a wall and getting ourselves into a bother. One more thing to do.

– what's that?

– see if they'll give you the money back for these.

– me?

– I think so, yes.

– could you?

– we'll both go.

———

The land has healing properties, and the tides can be applied like a leech to draw out poisons, maybe. But Peter sits in his kitchen, set apart from the earth and sea and the sureness of himself, and doubts if these things were ever sure at all. When the telephone rings he's not surprised to hear Brenda's voice; he almost believes that he draws her words fatefully down the line.

– Peter! Hello. I want to take the boys tomorrow.

– take them?

– for tea or something. You know. Christ, any objections?

– no objections.

– what's the matter with you?

– nothing. Is that all?

– no, it isn't, as a matter of fact. They'll be staying with me in the holidays.

– staying with you?

– I just said that.

– not: can they? Or: would it be all right?

– oh, if that's quite all right with you, of course. They are my children too.

– I hadn't noticed.

– what?

– nothing. What about them?

– what about them?

– what do they want? Where will they sleep, anyway?

– they won't be at my place. We'll be at Gerry's.

– ah.

– Gerry's very generous to them.

– I know.

– that's settled, then. Tell them we'll see them tomorrow after lunch.

———

At midday he calls the children to the table, reminding Danny to wash his hands. He bows his head for a moment in thanks for the food. He pours tea and adds extra milk to Danny's to cool it; he slices bread and they help themselves to bread and butter and eggs from the big red hen which are boiled and warm in the bowl. He asks Danny four times to eat with his mouth shut and twice to take his elbows off the table. In his head he sees horses pulling his limbs in different directions and knows that soon everyone will see the split.

The boys clear the table and Danny runs outside and Patrick upstairs. He calls them back and says oh nothing and then says goodbye. He takes yesterday's wage packet from his coat pocket and three bills from the Toby jug and divides the money between the envelopes. He lifts the oilskins from the hook and folds them into a canvas bag, adding a sweater, a woolly hat and a towel. He checks that the £10 is still in his pocket from the return of the chocolates. Then he swings the bag over his shoulder, wheels the bicycle out of the shed and rides away.

eighteen

In the bedroom Patrick lies on his bed with a book; Tintin and his dog run through the pages. Outside Danny stalks through the long grass waiting for a big black car, while in her room Aunt Elsa sleeps the sleep of the night walker.

In town Mrs Pickery sorts out the ironing while her husband watches the 2.30 at Doncaster. Mr Chandramohan stocks up his fridge; Franklin and Johnny Hamon sleep in their chairs after a liquid lunch and Michael studies a catalogue of bathroom suites. All over the island men move up and down their greenhouses and lift their lobster pots and mow their lawns. They watch the afternoon sport and drive towards tearooms that smell of cigarettes and chips. Saturday afternoon.

Brenda and Gerry arrive sometime after three. Who's watching the time? Nobody yet. They step into the hall and Gerry runs a finger over the clock. Danny clatters in.

– hi, Danny! Guess where we're going.

– his house!

– not today.

– when are we going to live with him?

– what's that?

– next week.

– they're not coming to live with me.

– you said!

– for the weekend, maybe. They're not going to live with me. Nobody is.

– want to! Want to!

– I don't have anyone live with me. Especially kids.

– just for the weekend to begin with, Danny.

– not beginning anything! I'm not taking over your kids so don't get any ideas. I don't like kids and I never will.

– Gerry!

– and if you think you can change me then you're making a big mistake.

Elsa is slowly descending the stairs. She holds her gown about her with one hand and pushes her hair with the other. Brenda feels a lid flip up and all the little devils fly out.

– I'm not letting the boys live in a house with her any longer.

– her?

– I know all about it.

– what do you know?

Danny looks from one to the other and makes a

strange animal noise. He calls for his dad. Patrick, standing in the doorway of his room and drinking in every word, drops the book from his hand. His dad. His dad said goodbye. He runs down, three steps at a time, pushes past the grown-ups in the hall and out of the door.

Past the wells and over the church wall is the quickest way. Through the churchyard and the hedge and the lane to the pine trees at the top of the hill and then down. Friday low water at five, clear the reef by three. Today low water six clear the reef by four. His watch says half past three just gone. Downhill his feet trip and skid under him and the cows slowly turn their heads. Brothers can't be separated we're not coming what do you think not if the law says otherwise keep it to yourself. Bye, son. Clear the reef by four. His watch says twenty to as he hits the flat road by the coast and the bay is hidden behind a hedge of tamarisk. His chest hurts as if it is packed with ice.

Over the sea wall he sees the orange buoy floating over the mooring. It's his job always to catch the rope with the boat hook as they drift in – he used to miss it out of nervousness but now he gets it every time. The Piqûre Rocks show their teeth against the sea; the Avaleur stands silhouette at the end of the cliffs.

The boy leans on the wall to catch his breath. There is no sign of the Nan, or of his father.

part two

dreams of fish

The artist must have sat in a boat a little way offshore, or imagined that he did. The lower half of the painting was of the sea, the sea until it reached the wall of black granite, the sea wall of the island. Above the wall the small white dwellings sat squat along the coast and spread over the hills. Below the wall in the deep water there was one fish, a very big one, swimming in an open-mouthed, uncaring fashion, from left to right across the canvas.

Of all the paintings stacked against the walls of his house (one of these same small white dwellings), she liked that one. When he held it up to the light he said that if he owned the whole island he would knock a hole in every roof and plant a tree in the foundations of every house. Then the trees would grow and grow towards the sun and push up the ceilings and crack open the walls and in time the hills would return to their own. That was his vision.

———

Across the road from his house Sarah de Garis is sitting now, where there is a gap in the wall and concrete steps leading down to the beach. There is no beach tonight because the tide is high; she sits down there on the steps as if she is hiding and the swell of the sea slides up and down the steps below, sucking and rolling, black and still. If a car should pass she would not want to be picked out in the headlights, but she need not hide, for there are no cars and the whole night is the same, black and still.

She is wearing a white nightshirt. She holds her hand flat against the wall on which the sun has shone since the morning, and the stone is warm. She is thinking of the fish. She can feel it passing by along the coast, a fish twenty, thirty, forty feet long, thunderously silent under the surface.

_____

On the east coast of England the shoreline is different. Small round grey pebbles are heaped in shelves; the tide-line is marked by crackling fingers of brown seaweed and squares of white polystyrene. The pebbles roll into dunes with the waves, but still they are grey. Behind them are the beach huts and the promenade where the wind blows; before them the sea sits without much heart, throwing out those little waves from time to time.

So it is on the east coast where the land is flat. This is not the deep Atlantic where a huge fish may pass; this is the North Sea and the lights of Harwich are a straight line winking in the dark.

The coast is different but the night is the same. The young girl would be down there on the beach but it is not allowed, so she watches at the window. She might go sometimes but not often, since she can't go unnoticed forever and she must keep her secret for the necessary times.

Her school fellows sigh and turn in their beds behind her. The clouds spread and spread again across the moon. There is no depth to the sea and she could wade right across to the level muds of Holland.

———

Sarah the child climbs down from the window and peers into the mirror. Her eyebrows are very dark in the moonlight. In the corner of the mirror she has pinned a postcard of the island, and its blues and greens show bravely in the thin air of this other place. She kisses the card and slips into her bed.

Sarah the woman stares out at the sea a while longer because she's not tired and she doesn't want shelter. The lights on the island show the bars and the hotels where she is not, and the moving headlights are cars in which she is not moving between one place and another. At last she stands, looking quickly up and down the road, and runs towards the third cottage from his and through her own front door. She could tear her skin off with her hands but she will not.

———

The bell begins to clang from the far end of the corridor.

– oh no. Tuesday. Double maths. Hockey. You awake, Sarah?

It's her friend in the next bed. Sarah murmurs; mm. She is awake and she does not want to move. The dormitory is cold. Five minutes more she wants to lie in her bed, listening to the water in the pipes. But the bell sounds louder as Matron walks along.

Beneath her tunic the vest and shirt feel awkward on her body as she sits at the breakfast table. Twelve girls sit at the table and twelve spoons dip into porridge; at the next table, twelve girls, at the next and the next. She doesn't hear the clattering of spoons. Through the window there's a glimpse of hedge and school wall and the brown North Sea reflects another morning with its mirror lies.

From the main house to the school buildings the girls walk two by two. Some straggle behind and run to catch up, grey cloaks flying in the cold east wind. Best friends naturally pair together. Sarah is wondering whether dark-haired people are tougher than blond. Miranda Thompson's white and freckled legs remind her, for Miranda is always unwell. And that Angela in the lower fifth, she looks almost albino and she is a sickly thing. Sarah has never heard of such a theory but still, the mind will ask its questions.

Her own self gives no clues. Her hair is a brown the colour of desks and floorboards, her nose is freckled; she is sometimes sick.

―――――

On the island, the adult Sarah unlocks the greenhouse at the far end of the row of greenhouses, and props the door open with a brick. This house needs clearing next and she will do it this morning, for the flowers in number three are tight and can be picked this afternoon.

The smell of earth and hay folds around her. She ties a scarf over her hair and begins to work.

Outside in the chicken run the hens gargle softly in their throats as they scratch the ground. Henny-Penny's head is pinker and more naked every day; the other hens will not stop pecking her. Inside, the weeds lift easily from the dry earth. Only the stems of the oxalis break, leaving their translucent pearls shining down in the soil. She forks them up, searching out the last, knowing how they multiply. Oh, this earth and its fine yellow dust, high up on the island and far from the sea.

―――――

Danny Duncan, grown into a man now, grunts in his sleep and reaches for his woman. She is gone, the pretty one, out somewhere under the sun which is already high in the sky. Well, she's on holiday; he will sleep until she comes back to make him some tea.

His cottage, this early summer morning, breathes too in its hundred-years sleep. Cool in its thick walls of granite and the mortar soaked through and through with salt. Under the floors the sand that once blew about in the marram grass now lies tamped down, solid and suffocated under the cement and the tarmac road. The waves that touch the sea wall leave other sands behind when the tide falls. On these she is lying, Melissa, the pretty one. A blanket, a book, and her little black shoes.

She will leave Danny alone for these first few days; his hunger for her will grow. It is her holiday and the sun shines.

———

The cloakrooms are dim and the air is chilly with leather and stone. Through the open door there are shouts from the hockey pitches under a washed-out sky. Sarah sits on her heels among the cloaks and she is still, finding a space between things which is safer than on the outside.

The pain for home is almost gone; eaten, swallowed down, and only the taste remains. The schoolgirls long for boys now instead of their mothers; it is easier to yearn collectively than separately. Each one confides the name of a boy from home, a talisman against the darkness of self. Photos are pressed into diaries with talk of first kisses.

Each homecoming to the island when she steps off the plane, her legs tremble. Each time the tears spill; it isn't even a happiness, only a swing of the pendulum. Her bed, her home, her place in the world so thirsted for, saying: come back and look at us and sit in us and sleep in us, and drop out of us again through the mesh.

– hello, funny face! Hobbsey missed you, you'll be for it tomorrow!

Sarah smiles and jumps up. Now she is one of them, girls changing their shoes, worrying over homework, friendships, spots.

———

In the midday blue a high tide covers the sand and a shadow passes. The reflections catch like so many windows, and an eye pivots slowly, this way, that. Or perhaps it is just a cloud. In the cottage he drinks his tea quickly now that it is cooled. He looks at Melissa sitting on the bed, then with one hand he peels back the towel that covers her big sweet breasts. The rhythms of life are simple; in and out, in and out.

In the greenhouse by the chicken run, the two front and centre beds are clear, except under the lights where the rain comes in and fresh weed grows. Sarah sits on the water pipe and pours tea into the lid of a flask. She will sleep tonight, surely.

When the tea is finished she leaves the flask on a shelf by the door. On the shelf there's a glove and two wire hooks and a length of pipe; they were there last week and will be there next week and this comforts her. She takes an armful of weed for the bonfire on her way to number three.

There are ten rows of the dark green leaves and their freesias. The flowers are perfect with their one opening bud. Yellow on the left, mixed on the right. She bends and picks and bends and picks for Covent Garden tomorrow morning and the hours pass as the surface of water over her head.

––––––

She's a schoolgirl studying a geography book and sometimes looking down on the road. The innocent road curves with the school wall and hedges and tennis courts where free people walk slowly along with their dogs and their shopping. There from the roof of the shed where the moss grows, she looks down.

Tonight after lights-out she can tiptoe to the washrooms and climb down the fire escape. In the dull yellow corridors she can run noiselessly down to the dining rooms and out through the window, dropping down into the soft flower bed. She can skip from darkness to darkness while the housemistress bends her grey head over a desk behind the glass. Climb the wall by the gatepost. On the beach her feet can scatter stones, beating the wet stones with her sandals, standing knee-deep in a sea which will not suck.

Ah, but it's no good. After supper she queues for the library and takes her books upstairs. She looks at the timetable for Wednesdays and tidies her clothes, filled with such a wanting that she knows, now, is just a wanting and not for anything she can name.

———

At five o'clock Sarah finishes work. She makes her way home along the back lanes where the yellow and white hedgerows are full of threat. From the high ground she zigzags downhill, past the farm where he played as a boy and across the fields where the magpies strut. Skirting the cottages as a rabbit feigns not to know the nearness of the burrow.

Filling the kettle she watches the movement of people along the coast. When Melissa walks by it fills her heart and stops her heart as the blonde curls toss in the breeze. Sarah would like to calm her and quieten her and cup her loveliness in her own hands. She discovers that love of a man is the love of his women too, extending past the point of the heart. To stop is to be jealous and to go on is a miracle of air and high altitudes. The smells and tastes and secrets touch a place further than their little lives; their blood is her blood, it is all the same. Melissa! But Melissa goes by and steps into his car and disappears.

The tide is out at sunset and the night-clouds over the land will pull the sea back up like a blanket. Sarah walks the low tide after the planet tips back from the sun. Rocks bare their pools for an hour where fish dart from her feet and crabs shuffle into the sand. In wet places the shells spiral and hiss, feeling the coming of the water. Sarah paces the tide. The aftertaste of pain is hugged to her stomach. If she belonged anywhere she would sink her pearls into the earth and the soft rain would come.

———

Danny the boy stole a horse from his uncle's farm, the same summer a body was found down a well by the old house. It wasn't really stealing if the beast wanted to canter down to the beach, and the broad grey back was a kingly mount. Quite sure of himself the boy opened the gate and crossed the stream and touched the warm neck, down to the slipway with the hooves on the cobbles, to wade into the ocean like some god.

Fishermen unhurried rowed their boats and turned the horse's head and shook their fingers at the boy: go home, rub the mare down and wash off the salt, mind now. And he obeyed them, but he knew that he would take his moments like this and not care.

———

In the dark of midnight Sarah lies in her bed. There are no more hours to spend daring the outside and walking the beach. The sea laps the wall and drives her in. Her house is a small white dwelling on the coast and behind its dark eyes she lies quiet and still, with the bruise of his love almost gone, eaten, swallowed down.

Three doors away his cottage glows with candlelight. He moves up and down and in and out of the woman, watching her fingers clutch the sheets. Next week after the spring tides he will start work on the roof and replace the joists that rot.

The sea rolls its stones and leaves them deeper than the waves can reach. With each thump of ocean the wall shudders and the dwellings toss in their concrete beds, so close to the switch of a great tail and the rhythmical breathing of gills.

part three

one

The church is never locked; the great iron ring always turns. It opens a small gate set into the heavy doors of the porch. The flagstones are cold. The church is full of the cold air of the hereafter.

Brenda lifts the latch on a little pew, and sits. She does not look up towards the altar or aim her prayers anywhere. But she seems to be praying. She is muttering something under her breath. Her hands clasp and unclasp in her lap.

The nave of St Stephen's church stands over her, dim and gracious. The family crests of old Port Victoria families can just be made out on the cloths hanging from the beams. The colours have faded to nothing, the threads eaten away by the passing of the years. They hang dead straight above her head.

She stirs, after a while. She retraces her steps and lets the door fall shut behind her. The gravestones lean back into the grass. She says something, a little louder this time.

– Wish they were all under there. Her. And him. And that bloody Hilda Pickery too.

She sets her lips into a straight line and walks past the gateposts and down the driveway to Les Puits. The curtains are drawn across the upstairs windows. In the jumble of the porch she sees that Peter's boots are missing; for a moment it seems that he must be at work this morning, as usual. But Peter took his boots with him when he left, two weeks ago.

She bangs the knocker against the door, sending the pigeons flying up from the roof. Again and again the noise echoes round the yard but no one comes to the door. Either Elsa sleeps like the dead or saw her coming and won't answer.

Brenda leaves the front door and opens the yard gate. She doesn't know whether or not the hens have been fed; she isn't interested in hens. She stands back and looks at the window she knows to be her sister-in-law's. She stoops to pick up a small pebble and sends it tumbling against the pane. Nothing happens. She lifts a sizeable stone and hurls it hard. The glass shatters inwards; tiny shards tinkle down towards the earth.

———

Port Victoria is not a big town. Even so, the summer is a breathless season in those streets, after the open fields. The boys haven't been back to Les Puits since their father left, they live under the little grey roofs of Turkenwell now, with their mother, closer to her than they have ever been before.

– get off that cushion.

– that's my cushion.

– it is not; it's mine.

– I sleep on it.

– yes, but it's mine. Now get off.

– why?

– Daniel, just get off. I need my skirt. Oh, look at that – it's all creased. Can't you look where you put things?

– I didn't.

– you put your cushion there.

– 's not my cushion you said.

– you know perfectly well what I mean. Cheeky little beggar. Henry'll just have to put up with me like this; I'm not changing again.

– why d'you go?

– got to earn money to feed you lot, haven't I.

– don't want you to go.

– don't start, Chrissake. Patrick, get your nose out of that book and listen. You listening?

– yes, mum.

– there's a quid for bread. Go to the park and get bread on the way back. For gawd's sake keep quiet – don't want her sticking her nose in again. Got that?

– yeah.

– and don't lose that money. Right then, I'm off.

She doesn't look the same now, walking along the road.

How can a body change its shape so, in a few weeks? It's not the shape that is different, but the flow.

Patrick and Danny wrestle in the cushions for a while in the empty flat. When they leave, the crashing of the front door behind them sends the next door flying open as if on a spring. Wilf Pickery has been waiting; he can get a word in before opening time.

– eeugh! Don't let me catch holda yer. End of the month an' yer out! Garn!

They skate down the steps, away from the park, down to the harbour. The sheet of water draws them; magnet-like it pulls the soles of their feet along the wharves. This is their playground, the crates and cranes and piles of timber. The sea wall is the tightrope, with safety on one side and the deep on the other.

———

There's Willy le Cras still sitting in the same place. Not so much time has gone by after all. Brenda slides a pint of mild towards him; wipes the froth off the bar.

– all right, Willy?

– aye.

– I'll leave you to it, then, nice an' peaceful. Henry – you got a moment?

– can it wait, love? I've got these invoices to do.

– Okay then.

She's tired; she could sleep for a week. It must be the worry. What's wrong, exactly? The boys, of course. What else – Gerry? Oh no, she's better off without him, isn't she? It's quite a relief, isn't it?

– wake up, darlin'.

– oooh! Me God! Don't do that; I'll die of fright.

– 'an I'll give yer the kiss o' life. Three pints, darlin'. Thanking you. An' crisps. Them vinegar ones. Any news from your lost love, 'ave yer?

– who?

– yer know – yer ancient mariner.

– nope.

– 'e must've arrived somewhere by now. Wherever 'e was going. Where was 'e going?

– I'm surprised you don't know, Franklin; you know everything else, doncha?

– yeah, mostly. I wouldn't ask, only 'e never did come about that Lister.

– the what?

– that engine, you know. Gone off without one, 'asn't 'e?

– I don't know. It's not my business, nor yours either.

– it's been running a helluva swell from the north, y'know.

– you want anything else? There's other people to serve.

– Okay, okay. Only showing an interest, like.

Mid afternoon and the doors are closed, the chairs stacked, the floors mopped. Brenda leans on a bar stool, picking her nails. She tells Henry that she's in a fix. The neighbours have complained about her boys in the flat; they say that it's in the lease: no children. The landlord's given them until the end of the month and then she'll have to take them back to the house in St Stephen's. It'll be too far for her to come into work twice a day from there. She's in a real fix.

– what about your family, love? Your parents?

– me mum's dead.

– and your dad?

– we don't speak.

– ah. Well. Look, you've got a couple of weeks; something might turn up; it usually does. I'd hate to lose you, Brend. I'd have to get someone else, you know – 'specially now, in the summer.

– I know.

– go on, then. There might be some good news waiting at home. See you tonight.

When a car drives up alongside, she almost thinks... but then a man in a white shirt opens the door, steps out and proffers his hand.

– Mrs Duncan?

– that's me.

– I'm Detective Sergeant Mullins. We've got a spot of trouble with your youngsters.

– *what?*

– nothing much to worry about, but if you'll just come with me... that's it. They're at the station.

– what they done?

– seems one of the dockers caught them tampering with some goods on the North Quay. Bit young to be on their own down there, aren't they?

– little blighters! I'll give 'em what for.

– they're with one of our women at the moment. She'll have a word with you. Here we are. This way, please.

two

Dear Susan,

I arrived in Cork last Friday. I was in Falmouth before that. The boat needs a few repairs. I am staying with my cousin Tom and his wife. Can you send me some news of the boys? I'm sure Brenda won't mind you seeing them sometimes. Tell Danny I'm sorry to miss his birthday and that I'll see you all soon.

Love,

Peter

Susan holds the letter in her hand. She feels wonder, and annoyance, and then concern. She reads it again. If the boys have a new life, then it can't be the one that their father imagines. Her mum goes on about nothing else now, on Saturdays. But it's not up to her to interfere, is it? He's got a cheek to ask, really. He never said goodbye or anything.

But then he says: I'll see you all soon. She looks at the envelope where he's written her name. Miss Susan

Pickery. Blue and clear and definite. She can see him, suddenly, in that old pullover he wears. Thank God he's safe.

She checks her watch. In twenty minutes the night staff will come in. She must remember to let them know that Mr Farthing isn't to have his drink at eight anymore; he can't keep it in at night. Was there anything else? Well then, she'll pop down to her mum and dad. She needn't actually show them the letter.

But Patrick and Danny – has he written to them? Do they know he's safe? She'll make sure that they do.

She parks the minibus at the top of The Steps and makes her way down. Lovely evening. She could take the boys down to the harbour, if they're allowed to stay up late.

Passing beneath the window of Number 5, she hears voices. Danny's unmistakable yell. Hurriedly she knocks on her parents' door.

– there! can you hear that? Listen to them!

– let me in, mum.

Through the passage and into the kitchen Hilda Pickery talks excitedly. Them next door were brought back today by a policewoman, just fancy! Thank goodness it was after closing time and Wilf was at home to see. When the policewoman left there'd been all hell let loose, by all accounts. Screeching and crashing about, even worse than now. But they're still at it – listen!

– I think I'd better go and see if I can do anything to help, mum.

– that's right – you do that, my girl. You see what's going on.

———

– What the hell do you want?

– oh. I'm Susan Pickery. I'm from next door. At least...

– I know who you are. Think I'm stupid? She sent you to poke your nose in too? Well you can fuck off.

– no she didn't. I came to say... well, I've had a letter. From Peter.

– oh, yes? I get it! Oh, that's very nice! Well you know where you can stuff it. Get out of my way; I'm late for work.

Brenda pushes past, banging the door behind her. Susan blinks, turns to go, then she returns to the door and softly knocks. She tries the handle.

– Patrick? Danny? It's me, Auntie Susan.

– we're not allowed to open the door. She'll murder us if we do.

– just open it a bit. Come on, Patrick. I don't want to talk too loud. Good lad. Are you okay?

– Yes...

– I've heard from your dad! He's fine. He sends his love. Oh, sweetheart...

The boy's shoulders pull up; his mouth trembles.

– oh my love, don't cry. This is just a bad patch; it'll get better. Honest it will...

– I was... we were... going to be with him – an' we

can't stay here – an' me mum... she...

   – shh. It'll come right. Come on, love. Where's Danny?

   – there. Under the bed.

   – I've got to go. Listen! I'll write to your dad. It'll come right, okay?

   – Auntie Susan?

   – yes, love?

   – we're ever so hungry.

three

Dear Peter,

Thank you for the letter. I have seen the boys and they are well. I'm not sure if you know but they are living with their mother and it's not my business but I think you should know. There's a bit of trouble and they must get out of the flat, the boys that is, I'm not sure about your wife. I'm glad you are well.

Love,

Susan Pickery.

———

– Miss Pickery? There's someone on the phone for you.

– thank you, nurse. I'm busy here. Who is it?

– Peter somebody. Duncan I think.

– Lord. I'm coming. Take over will you?

– hello?

– Susan?

– yes – Peter?

– I'm in a phone box; can't be long. I got your letter. What's going on? Where are the boys?

– oh Peter; I haven't seen them. They're still in the flat in town, I think. My mum says they're moving out at the weekend, going back to your place...

– where's my sister? I've been ringing and ringing.

– I don't know.

– who's going to look after them?

– I don't know.

– I'm arranging something with the bank. Susan, I've had an idea. I know it's a lot to ask – wait, the money – you still there?

– yes.

– could you bring them here – is there any way? Can you take a holiday? I'll send you the money. Susan?

– oh I don't know. I don't know what to say. You mean in a plane?

– yes. Susan, will you think about it? Can I ring you tomorrow?

– yes.

– great. I really miss them, you know.

———

Brenda comes out of the bank manager's office feeling so relieved that suddenly she has to sit down. At least one thing has been taken care of. She'd been so worried about money it was making her quite dizzy. Now the bank fellow has explained how Peter's going to release the South Field for sale to the Corbins, like they always wanted, and when the sale goes through she'll get the money, for the children.

Now she can keep the flat, even if she has to take the boys to St Stephen's for a while. She'll move back as soon as she can. There's no way that she, Brenda Duncan, is going to be stuck out there in St Stephen's for long with that cow of a sister-in-law. Not a chance.

And after the South Field there's always the Long Meadow. It's only a bit of grass, but someone'd buy it. She doesn't need to worry about money. Peter'll come back for the boys soon enough, anyway. He'll come running back.

———

– You'll do no such thing.

– I might, mum. It's not the end of the world.

– Ireland? It might as well be. I never heard of such an idea!

– the boys aren't old enough to travel on their own – Peter thinks they should be with him.

– Peter, is it, now? It was Mr Duncan last week. You're playing with fire, mark my words.

– oh, mum! He's not like that.

– he's a man, ain't he? He wants you to take his kids to him, does he? And do a bit of cooking. And The Other Thing. You're not to go.

– I'm not asking you, mum. I'll make up my own mind.

Mrs Pickery looks at her daughter very hard.

– you'll rue the day, my miss. Pass me that other bag. I can manage now, thank you.

Susan drives away with her heart thudding. She's never spoken back to her mother like that before. Usually she helps with the shopping and then stays for tea, and she might have seen Patrick and Danny – they could be moving out today, this very minute. Now she's driving away and missed her chance.

She'll have no news to tell Peter. She'll just tell him yes, she'd love to come if he needs her. He does need her. It's a bit sudden, though. He wasn't a man to rush anything, before all this. Things never seem to work out if they're done in a rush. Maybe her mum's got a point. It doesn't feel right, somehow, going to him. He'd come to her, wouldn't he, if it was right? Perhaps she won't get any time off work. That's what she'll say. She'll just tell him no.

———

It's Sunday morning and the old station wagon is bowling along past the airport. Franklin, Johnny and Brenda are once again wedged in the front, with the boys in the back between bags and coils of rope, leaning out of the windows and screwing up their eyes into the wind.

Brenda turns her head as they pass the crossroads, looking down the road towards Le Clef du Ferme, but there is only a blur of trees. They leave the main road where it curves towards the west coast, following the narrow lane. Brenda shouts directions into Johnny's ear. At last they rattle down the drive of Les Puits, skidding to a halt outside the porch and raising a little puff of dust.

– there you are, madam; right to yer own front door. Don't say I never do nothin' for yer.

– 'ell! Take a look at it, will yer? 'S enormous! Coo! The 'eavenly choir an' all!

– blast. I forgot it was Sunday. That's morning service. The whole bloody parish'll know I'm here. Come on you lot, get out then. Oi! Daniel Duncan, come and help with them bags! Where's he gone?

– give 'em ere. We'll 'ave a squint inside. It's locked. You got a key, you?

– yeah, somewhere. Here. I'll do it. Patrick, bring that box. Don't stand there gawping.

The air inside reminds her of the church, cold and still as stone. She lights a cigarette.

– give us one. Reckon we deserve a cup of tea, don't you?

– jeez. Hang on a minute. Let me catch my breath. The Aga's out.

– don't look as if anyone's been 'ere fer a while, do it? Where's yer, y'know – yer mad sister-in-law?

– hush your big mouth. There's kids about. How should I know?

– nothin' in the fridge, any'ow. Want a lift to the shop? Got plenty time; pubs shut today, ain't they?

– an' the shop. Patrick'll go round the Corbins' later. It's okay. We're okay now.

– sure you'll be aw'right then, is it?

– yeah. Thanks, eh? I'll see you.

In the silence when they are gone, the stone cold fingers seem to circle her neck. She's going as nuts as Elsa, right enough. She crushes the cigarette into the floor and calls for Patrick.

– what?

– don't you *what* me. Come 'ere.

– yes, mum?

– where's Danny?

– he's gone off.

– well, take these up. And go and have a look in your aunt's room.

– must I?

– yes, whyever not? I'm not feeling so good; I'll come up later.

Patrick goes into the bedroom which he has always shared with Danny. It is as they left it – the books under the bed, the crayons on the floor. He inhales the familiar smell. Then he drops the bags and continues down the passage.

Nobody ever goes into Aunt Elsa's room. It is surrounded by privacy and he can almost feel the fabric of its veil. Now in the emptiness of the house the little landing outside her door is fairly humming. The hair prickles on his scalp. There might be a body in there. She might have fallen across the bed with a dagger in her and one arm dangling over the side, like that man in the picture, only he was in the bath.

He knocks. That's silly; dead people can't answer. He turns the handle, pushes the door. Nothing. His eyes take a quick look, nothing.

four

Now that they're home, there's nothing much to do. A thousand things, but nothing. Patrick, on that first day, feels some of the weight of those cold fingers.

He tells his mother that his aunt's room is empty, and then she shooes him outside. He walks listlessly around the yard and finds the hens gone. He goes to the Corbins' for bread and milk and is told that the hens escaped into the Long Meadow and a dog killed two. They put the others in a run behind their sheds. Danny is at the Corbins'; Auntie Debs says he can stay for tea but Patrick had better go home and tell his mother not to worry.

At the table in the kitchen Patrick silently wolfs down bread and jam and tinned peas. He told Auntie Debs that there was food in the cupboard but there was only jam and peas and custard powder. It's nice to hear the doves wobbling their throats up there on the roof.

He looks up quickly at his mother. She's ever so different all of a sudden. She always dressed sharp, like a series of boxes all magically balanced together. Now she's gone blurry. She's just sitting there looking at the old newspapers, lighting one cigarette off the end of the last one.

– what are you staring at?

– nothing.

– when you go back to school?

– next week.

Slowly through the week, he finds his way back into the feel of the house. The stones of the walls shift and settle into place, adjusting to the absence of his father and the fresh air blowing through the broken window into the empty room of his aunt. His mother said to leave the glass where it is. She sleeps in his father's bed. She sleeps and sleeps and sleeps.

Walking through the country lanes gives him back a rhythm and arranges his thoughts. First: who broke that window? Burglars took Aunt Elsa away or an alien force. Either way it is just as well, as his mother says she could never bear the bitch. Auntie Deb's dog is also a bitch.

His mum is a problem. Last night when the phone rang she screamed at it and pulled it right out of the wall. He'd best keep out of her way.

Then, his dad. Auntie Susan said he'd sent his love and his dad meant it. He meant love. So he'll come back. He'd come and find mum in his bed and wake her up with a kiss like she was a princess. If it was a question of waiting, then Patrick thought he could manage that.

Meanwhile he was walking to the shops and he could fill up the kitchen shelves again and make things come right.

———

Les Puits affects Brenda like a sickness, like vertigo. She can't stand it. The bloody birds in the roof stink. She can't pin her mind on anything. At least the kids are out of her hair; they're out getting up to no good, dawn till dusk.

In her dreams she leaves the house quietly, squeezing the front door behind her without a sound. She hurries down the lane hearing footsteps behind her. It's Gerry. She dodges and turns, but he is always there; he won't be shaken off.

She decides to go to his house. He's put the bad eye on her, and that's not all. She takes the number eleven bus as far as the crossroads, and then walks. She senses, before she reaches Le Clef, that he is not there. Sure enough, there's no sign of life. The lawns are parched and yellow and the flower beds powder dry.

Sitting on the bus on the way back to Les Puits, she changes her mind. She stays in her seat for two more stops and gets off at the Vine Farm. They'll know. She'll find out today, if it kills her.

At the farmhouse door, Jack's wife Biddy wipes her hands on a dishcloth and eyes Brenda carefully. Ah yes, she knows about this one.

– my husband will be in just now. He's always in for his dinner, twelve sharp. It's him you're wanting?

– yes. Or Simon.

– our Simon's taking a tractor to Deborah's place and he'll take his dinner there. He took over your husband's job, temporarily, like. He's college educated, not a farm worker. 'Ere comes Jack now. Look who we've got here, mon vieux.

– oh aye. Just wait 'til these boots is off. Our Peter's wife, isn't it? Let me wash my hands.

– will you stay and have a spot of dinner? Only we can't wait; he only has the hour. You sure? Cup of tea then; come on, sit down. She's asking after our Simon.

– not Simon really... It's Gerald I want to get hold of. You know Gerald.

– oh aye. Aye. Spent a bit of time together, they have, on and off.

– Gerald's gone back to London, didn't he say? Our Simon's helping us now – I was telling the young lady – since Peter left.

– and he left mighty suddenly, y'know. Not like him at all, was it? Not at all. One day he says he wants a long leave and can Simon take over for a while and I says yes, he's not settled into anything over here yet. And he asks how soon can Simon start and I say anytime, and the next thing we know he's gone.

The gravy running over the potatoes is making Brenda feel sick. She holds on to the tablecloth.

– we can't keep his job open indefinitely. Our Simon's applied for a position in the bank. We need a permanent man; the potatoes keep growing. You all right, are you?

– yes; it's hot in here. I have to go now. It's okay. You needn't come to the door.

– it's polite. So you're back in St Stephen's, is it? We'll be seeing you in church, then.

Brenda walks away rapidly. That Biddy Vine looks at me as if she knows. She's a right nosy so-and-so.

———

Dear Brenda,

I heard you're back in the house. I phoned every day and the phone people say its out of order, is the bill paid? Mr Carmichael at the bank says you're getting the money all right, so please pay the phone. John and Deborah say they don't see you. I'm working with Tom, that's my cousin, in his boatyard for now. It's good work but if you and the boys need anything you just say. I'll wait to hear from you then,

Love,

Peter

———

In the soft early morning of September Patrick wakes up and turns over in his bed. Danny stays over at the Corbins' some nights now and it's an unexpected wonder to have a room to himself; something that has never happened before.

He watches a spider edge along the top of the wall. Dad said they come into the house in September to lay their eggs. It's nice when that happens – when you know something, and its true. He's never seen spider eggs.

Three days left of the holidays. He could stay in bed; his mum probably will. She's getting like Aunt Elsa; he hears her in the kitchen in the middle of the night. Maybe all women get like that. It's a phase. When Danny kept wetting his pants last year they said it was a phase.

He'll get up, though. He's found a great place for crabs. It's down by the moorings at the end of the Piqûre – you can only get to it on a big low tide. Like in about an hour. He pads across the room, finding his clothes, half aware of the breeze stirring the elms outside, happy to be home.

————

In the mid morning, Danny Duncan walks in at the back door, which is open. The house is still; he hears the clock clicking quietly to itself. On the hall table there is a square white envelope. He picks it up; the handwriting looks familiar. He pushes it into the little slit between the table and the wall, tucking down the last white corner until it can't be seen at all.

five

– Danny! get back in 'ere.

– why?

– do as you're told. Quick. Get in. I don't want that lot coming out of church looking at us over the wall. Who were you talking to?

– Auntie Debs.

– what was she saying now?

– she says not to go to her place 'cos of the surprise she was makin' yesterday and she's bringin' it now when she's got the dinner in.

– bringing what?

– the surprise.

– *hang*. Patrick! Get those dishes off the table. I'm going upstairs.

Deborah Corbin is a sensible woman. She is still dressed in her church clothes, a cotton two-piece and good brown shoes. She carries something carefully balanced on a plate. Behind her comes her daughter, wearing a pretty dress, stopping to pluck a handful of grass for the horse as they pass the field. Brenda watches as they approach.

– let them in, then.

– hello? Ah, you're here. Happy birthday to you, happy birthday to you, happy birthday dear Danny, happy birthday to you!

They stare at her. Brenda looks at Patrick and they both look at Danny, who keeps his eyes fixed on the plate. Under a lace cloth is a chocolate cake.

– it's just a little something. Five years old, eh? Don't they grow up quick? Our Lissa'll be seven just before Christmas. Shall I put it over here?

– yeah.

– starting school Tuesday, too! My, my. They can all walk along together. That's nice. Where are you off to, Melissa?

– just going out with Danny.

– oh no, not in that nice dress. Can you go upstairs a minute? All of you. I'd like a word, Brenda, if you don't mind. Peter's phoned, and he's a bit worried, you know. What's the matter with your phone?

– we don't have a phone.

– what do you mean?

– look, it's nice of you to bring a cake, I'm sure, but I'm not needing visitors, thank you. If Danny's a nuisance at your place you just send him back sharp.

– he's no trouble. He and Lissa are company for each other. Can't we arrange a time for Peter to speak to the boys at our place then?

— leave it alone, will you? Hey, you lot! Auntie Deborah's just leaving. Say thank you, Danny.

— thank you.

— all right. We'll see you soon. Bye, Patrick. Come on, Melissa.

———

She doesn't need visitors. It is more than that; she's withdrawing into her skin. Fishermen on the coast sleep lightly and attribute it to their cottages, built on sand. You might think that up on the broad back of Port Victoria, over the island's heart, the sleepers burrow into its soft inner core in their dreams. But Brenda plies into veins of metal. She opens her eyes with the taste of it in her mouth.

The nights and days run into each other; for her the world of awake and asleep are merged at their edge. She looks across the room towards the window where the darkness outside presses against the house. She listens to a car driving slowly past; the headlights arching a pattern of light up the walls and across the ceiling. The car turns at the end of the lane, and passes again.

She hurries downstairs, pulling on a gown. Out of the door she runs and along the drive to the gateposts, where the moon gleams on the black tarmac road.

Of course — they've lured her out of the house and now they are inside, waiting for her. She runs back and locks the door, rushing from room to room, flinging open doors and cupboards, checking every corner, turning on every light. No one.

She leaves by the back and tugs at the gate by the hen house. It resists her where the weeds have grown through the bars; it takes a minute to free the rope that ties it to the fence. She loops the rope over again, loosely, so that it still seems secure. She can escape that way now.

In the hall she sits down, her heart thumping. Behind her, the letter from Peter... 'if you need anything...' nestles against the wall. She turns off the light so that she can't be seen through the keyhole. Oh God. Oh God, she prays, don't let them come for me.

six

In September the blackberries have not fulfilled their promise. The harvest in the hedges dries up before it grows plump. The rains are late, and the wind blows dust over the hard red fruit.

The children walk to school. Patrick makes no attempt to walk with the others, but he worries when he hears them quarrel. It makes Danny drag behind, and he's too small to be by himself. What if a lorry comes round the corner and Danny should step out in front of it? Patrick paces his distance carefully, making it look as if he's just walking, as if he doesn't care.

At school nobody's said anything, and they don't need to. He knows Melissa's tongue. He hasn't even said anything to himself. A fact is a fact. He can't be sure.

The best thing in the world has happened, anyway. A letter from his dad. He knows it off by heart. *Dear Patrick/ How are you, son/I hope you're fine and Danny too/I heard you're all back home/that's good/I think of you often/ work hard at school/take care of your mother/I'll see you soon/I love you/Dad.*

It's great because it arrived on Saturday when he was alone in the kitchen. He took it right from the postman's hand. He keeps it in his inside pocket all day and under his pillow at night. Danny hasn't seen it; not even his mother. It's the best thing in the world.

———

As October becomes November, Deborah Corbin also wonders if a fact is a fact after all, and if they ought to tell Peter. It's hard to repeat what other people are saying when you want to keep out of that sort of thing. But the sale of the South Field has gone through, and he did say something about the Meadow; he'll phone again, most likely, this week or next. She mentions it to her husband.

– you can't say anything to him.

– you don't think it's true.

– I can't say, can I? I never see the woman, and if I did... well, I don't know, you can't go spreading talk. What's Peter to do?

– he could come back. He's fretting to see those boys. He's anxious not to upset things, I think. Maybe I should tell him that the coast is clear.

– you do as you think fit, my love. I don't have a mind for these things.

———

The rain has come; the evenings draw in, fast and dark. Patrick keeps the Aga going; he's learned its little ways. Turn the dial down at night, up in the morning, riddle the ash into the pan. Take the ash out when the wind's not blowing; cover the ash pit with a bit of soil.

He's out there with a spade when the Hamons' station wagon turns into the drive. The soil is wet and leafy on the spade, the rooks are cawing in the elms. Once, he would have run inside to find his mother and say; someone's coming! Not now. He likes it out here with the wet leaves and the rooks; he's finding his own place. Let her find hers.

It's not Franklin and Johnny but Michael and Louise who step out of the wagon and look around. Michael blows a stream of smoke into the air. Come on, he says to Louise.

Brenda is upstairs, lying down. She eases herself slowly off the bed and looks out of the window. Bugger them, she thinks. She'll have to go down. That lot will never go away until she does. What do they want now?

– oh, it's you.

– yeah, 's only us. Cor, you live far, hey, Brend? We 'ad a right time finding it. Brought you some mack'rel. Present from the lads.

Brenda looks at Louise. Louise, whom she's only seen once or twice last summer, a young whip of a girl. Now she comes in here all bursting out of her coat.

– 'lo, Brend. We come to invite you to the weddin',

didn't we, Michael? It's Sat'day next.

-yeah, well. I'll leave you ladies to it. Gonna check the oil.

Louise looks at Brenda just as carefully. She isn't asked to sit down, but she does.

– you ain't showin' much.

– who told you?

Louise lets out a little sigh.

– come on, Brend. You know what this island's like. I ain't come to have a ding-dong with you. When you expectin'?

– February.

– thought so. Same as me, see. We could be in the Nursing Home together. Only it's my first, so I might be late. Blimey, you'd never know you're nearly seven months gone. You don't look no different. Look at me – I'm blown up like a whale. You been sick much?

– yeah.

– and me. Only at first, though. Want a fag?

– yeah, go on.

– shouldn't really, but I can't stop. Don't it feel peculiar when it moves about?

There is a long silence.

– pity you don't live in town no more. We could see each other a bit. What are you going to do, then? After, like.

– I'm going to drop it down the well.

– oh Christ almighty! Oh don't say such things – it's

bad luck. You are funny, Brend. My sister gets a bit like that. You'll love it when you see it, though. She always does.

   – you ready, Louise?

   – coming.

   – sorry we can't stay, like, Brend. Got the tackle in the back. We're doing a run off the Point after tea.

   – it's all right, Michael. Thanks for the fish. Say hi to the boys.

   – yeah. We miss yer in the pub an' all. New barmaid's a bit of a sourpuss. Are yer comin' Saturday?

   – I don't know.

   – ah well. See you then.

   – see you, Michael. Bye, Louise.

Brenda sits down. Don't those fish look funny, with their tails hanging off the draining board. Don't they look funny up here in this tomb, instead of moving about, busy in the sea.

seven

Waiting his turn to step down from the plane, Peter Duncan is reluctant to plant his feet on the island again. Who would have thought it? He has been so hungry to see his children that he hasn't paused to examine his own returning self. The outer self has changed – he's thinner, he has grown a beard. The sides of it are grey.

It's his legs that feel reluctant to propel him forward now, down the steps. Come on legs; we're going home.

A thin east wind nips his ankles as he waits for a taxi. Weather's the same, anyway. Deborah said – well, she said a lot, and hinted at more, and it was true, the bit about Les Puits being his home. He's been six months away, and he'll see.

It is all just the same. The main road still slides away down to the coast – the sky is black on the horizon. He'd be checking the mooring now, if the Nan were here, but she's safe in her berth in Cork harbour. So he is not slipping back in time; there's a real live boat rocking gently on the water somewhere else and she is his home, too.

It is only the lanes rolling back, not the months. He's a free man. He's going to sort out a few things.

There is the shop. There's the sign that says open when it's closed. There are Andy Gavey's cows. There are the pine trees. There's the church and the gateposts.

There's...

He opens the taxi door and his arms and his heart wider than wide and his great grown son hugs him high up his chest almost at his shoulders. Patrick's face is red and bright and he can't speak; they stand there grinning and laughing, and after a while he notices the taxi driver waiting and blowing on his hands.

It smells the same, the house. Couldn't say of what, but the smell shafts into his being. In the kitchen she is standing awkwardly by the table. She moves towards him. It's true, then.

———

– Danny said he'd be here. He'll be on his way.

– ah, one at a time, is it? Gives me a chance to see you properly. You look so... you've grown up somehow, lad. Brenda. You all right?

– I've grown an' all. As you can see.

– yes.

– Dad, can I make tea? Look, kettle's on the hob already.

– grand. That's grand. A real treat. Where's Danny, you say?

– he'll be to Deborah's. He's there more often than not.

– Patrick, you great giant – while that tea's drawing, won't you nip over and fetch him for me? And tell your Aunt Debs I'll be calling soon. In a day or two, tell her.

– yes, Dad. Dad?

– yes?

– it's wonderful. Your beard – and everything.

———

– Brenda.

– go on, say it.

– no. Nothing, really. Takes a bit of getting used to, coming back and seeing you here.

– I had to. I couldn't stay in the flat with the kids.

– Deborah said.

———

At teatime they sit together at the kitchen table. Last time they all did so, Danny wasn't even big enough for a high chair, Peter recalls. He used to feed him sops on his knee after Brenda went, and leave him with Elsa when he went to work. There was a pram and a playpen. He must have been all right. Doesn't seem to have done him any harm. Look at him now, bright as a button, tucking into those chocolates. Kids don't seem to be affected by anything much.

Danny's quick eyes dart from person to person, working it out. When he's bigger, no one will get the better of him, no one.

– best leave a few of those, eh, Danny?

– you said they were mine.

– so they are. Isn't it best to leave some for tomorrow? Ah, well. What time do you boys go to bed nowadays?

– anytime.

– Ah. Saturday tomorrow. Tell you what. You go to bed early tonight, and tomorrow we'll fix up the kite first thing, and fly it if there's still a wind, okay?

– I want to fly it first. It's mine.

– you shall.

– come on, Dan. Thanks for the book, Dad.

– you having baths? Right. I'll come up and say goodnight later. And Patrick – you make a bloomin' marvellous cup of tea.

———

In the dark, Patrick's bed is a boat. On it he is sailing with the wind of this new turn of events. His dad is back in the house; he may go or he may stay, but for now they are gathered under one roof. Prayers work.

Downstairs Peter sits in his chair. Here is the chair and the washing hanging above the Aga and the balls of fluff in the corner. The distances between one thing and another have subtly altered; as an artist he could perhaps close one eye and extend his thumb and see the shifting of perspective. Something is bigger, or smaller, around the chair and the corners of the room and himself.

He is warm from Patrick's embrace. The guilt of leaving him – ah, now he sees it. He sighs. That was the reluctance he felt; had he done a great wrong, or hadn't he? From Patrick at least, he has been granted absolution. Danny is probably too young to understand.

This woman sitting in the chair opposite, her face hidden over a newspaper, her body tense. That body flavoured now by the chemistry of Gerald Vine. His wife.

– you never answered my letter.

– I never got any letter.

He clears his throat; starts again.

– any news of Elsa?

She relaxes a little, lowers the paper, shakes her head. She tells him about the broken window; it was her, a mistake; it was nothing.

– you say that was the middle of August? She's been gone since before then, then. Long time. She never was one for letters, mind. Nor the telephone, for that matter.

The wind will be blowing all right for kite-flying tomorrow, you can bet. Listen to it whushing down the flue – whumph, whumph. Brenda speaks vaguely, almost talking to herself.

– she would have left the same time he did, you see. They would have gone together.

– he? You mean...? I didn't know. I don't know anything.

– well you wouldn't, would you. He went, and she went. Like you went.

I only went because you left *me*, remember.

– does he know...

– no! Not from me, anyhow. Probably he does, though. People know everything don't they – 'cept you.

She interrupts his next words with a wave of her hand.

– I've been sleeping in your room.

My room? Not *our* room, no, I suppose not. What does she mean? Is she offering to move out?

– there's Elsa's room, I suppose.

For her? For me?

– no, I'll sleep down here, on the couch. I used to, you know.

The air is loaded with the words unsaid. I couldn't bear to sleep upstairs without you. You left me first, let's not forget.

– I'm going up, then. I don't sleep so well.

Ah. Shame. I know what it's like.

Alone downstairs with the plink, plink of the tap and the susurration of the clock, he chides himself for his meanness. She cupped her hand under her belly when he spoke those last words, as she used to when it was Danny she was carrying, when they used those same niggardly, defensive voices. She's got reason to be defensive now, God knows. From his heart a little of the old blood seeps.

He opens the little black well on top of the Aga and shakes in some coal. He must get the phone fixed. There'll be plenty of jobs to do around the place. He pulls the couch across from the corner, nearer to the warmth; spreads out a blanket, shakes a cushion. It's not those jobs so much that he must do, it's that question of absolution. He left them all – Jack, Deborah, John, the Vauquiers. Susan. Something was skimped, badly finished. He doesn't feel so much of a free man with all that to square up.

eight

She's not the same in the morning. She has absorbed vitriol overnight. He remembers this now with horrible clarity, these silences and quick retorts; he was caught off guard by her complaisance yesterday.

– how long has the well been like that?

– like what?

– the big one, with the pump. The cover's off.

– ask the kids.

– they wouldn't go there. I've never let them. It's dangerous.

– listen to you! Why should you care, all of a sudden?

– don't be like that.

– don't be, don't be. It's *my* fault, is it?

– of course not. The wood is rotten. I'll fix up something on the top of it for now.

He takes the hen house door off its hinges and carries it to the well. He cuts new notches and secures it with stones. It won't last long. He must ask which of them was meddling around here. He looks back at the house. There are slates loose on the roof; he'll get up there later. When the wind drops. The whole place could do with a coat of paint. He shakes his head.

– Dad!

– he's spoiled my kite. He's broke it.

– I didn't mean to. I nearly got it right.

– what's happened? Come and spread it out where I can see. It's a crosspiece, isn't it? We'll find a bit of dowling around. Look in the shed, will you? About this long.

He calls Brenda but she will not come. They stand in the meadow with frozen ears and stiff fingers and the patched kite, trying to coax it into the air. The wind lifts it up and dumps it down, over and over. One more try, he urges. Hup! The kite twirls and jerks away like a mad thing, and drops into the top of the elms.

– can you believe it! That's bad luck. P'raps we can get it. Is the ladder still there by the wall? Hey, where you going, Dan? Where's he off to?

– jus' going.

– well, not now. It's my first morning home.

– fuckin'ell.

– I beg your pardon, young man...

– fuckin'ell.

– go into the house and up to your room; don't come down 'til you've mended your language.

Oh, and there are slates off the roof, and the house needs a coat of paint.

———

The man and the woman sit in the kitchen. It is a large kitchen, with a couch in the corner. You can touch the air that generations have touched in the close pores of the stone, the weave of the wood in the beams, in and out.

The man and the woman both have newspapers on their laps. He is not reading his; rather, he lets his gaze fall on her and away quickly and back again. She is sitting like a brittle bird, her wrists thin, her fingers tight on the paper's edge. Then again, she is not bird-like. In her compactness she seems rather to be in her coils, ready to spit.

– who will look after you then, when your time comes?

– I'll go to the Nursing Home, won't I?

– in your flat, you can't have... children.

– I'm not keeping it. I'll give it away.

He speaks precisely, carefully.

– are you sure?

– yes.

– have you arranged it?

– no.

– there are arrangements... papers...

– I don't know about that...

– the adoption agency...

– no.

– you must.

– I don't know how.

For a moment he thinks he will take it, as his own. Her children are his children. He'll keep them here, everyone. She guesses his thoughts.

– I'm not keeping it. I don't want it. I hate it.

Silence.

– I hate it.

– I'll find out about adoption.

– I don't want to see anyone.

– I'll do what I can.

———

The kitchen at the Corbins' exudes a different breath. It's a granite farmhouse of the same age, low lying, a creeping thing petrified on the valley lip. But inside it's all modern; a bright light welcomes Peter as he steps through the back door on Sunday morning after church, straight into the clatter of family, radio, dogs, a cup of tea.

– it's good to be here – thanks, Deborah, I will. Just the one, please.

– you've picked up a bit of the accent on the other side, eh?

– is it? Well, you should hear some of them; I can't always be understanding them.

– there you go again!

– you've a good job, then? Boatyard, you said?

– that's right. It's something different. Pay's all right, when there's work. There's nothing at the moment. Big job coming up in January.

   – and it's yours, is it?

   – if I want it.

   – and you do.

   – you know, John – it's funny. I never thought I'd be anywhere but here. Home, and all. But over there it's like... I can't say. Like...

   – I can see how it might be. No memories, like.

   – something like that.

   – and you can stay with your cousin?

   – for now. There's room.

The two men sit at the table: Deborah moves behind them, peeling, chopping, moving pans.

   – you know about Brenda.

   – we don't know much.

   – she wants the baby adopted. She won't stay in the house. Says she's got enough friends in town to care for her.

   – what do you want?

   – it's no odds. I can't stop her.

   – maybe: you'll be staying yourself then, with the boys?

   – I've given it thought. I reckon I'll take them with me, back over there. At least for a while: see how it goes. We've been asked for Christmas. I think it might be best for them, to be away.

   – you mean there'll be talk, with the baby.

   – there's already talk, no doubt.

   – there is. She'll take it hard, in town.

– she doesn't care.

The dog pricks up its ears for a moment, but there are only familiar sounds. It's just Melissa, there behind the door.

– you'll have some tea with us, Peter?

– thanks, no. I'd best get back. You still interested in the Meadow, is it?

– we are. The herd's increasing; we'll need the extra water, come summer. So it's the wells we'd want, mostly. Then again, they go with the house, wouldn't they?

– they've been out of use since I was a nipper. Don't see why you shouldn't have the use of them – I'll look out the papers. Elsa has a half share – not that she has any interest in it, mind. She gave me the legal rights to the surrounding land and verges.

– no word from her?

– not yet.

– not sending out a search party?

– I wondered, you know, if something'd happened. But she left her things all sorted out, like she planned to go for some time. Brenda thinks... well, Brenda thinks she's on the mainland. I'll find out if I can act in her absence. Bob Vauquier – he'll know.

nine

– where's Danny?

– haven't seen him.

– Patrick! Danny up there with you?

– no...

– fetch him, will you? And get your hands washed for tea.

Peter is scrambling eggs. They're sticking to the pan. The Aga's too hot, or maybe he's using the wrong pan. Brenda won't be eating with them; she takes wedges off the bread and biscuits out of the tin when she's on her own. Peter thinks he can smell alcohol on her, but he can't be sure. Only the cold in the upstairs rooms drives her down here to the kitchen.

– I can't find him.

– he'd not be over the way now, would he? Honestly, what a time to go. It's blowing all hell out there. Uh! I'll have to leave this. I'll go, Patrick; it's dark. Done your hands? Watch the toast! I'll be back in a minute.

It's gusting from the west; it'll bring rain. He should have fixed those slates while there was a lull this morning. He hunches into his coat. The boy spends too much time over there.

– no, we've not seen him all day. Melissa was over to you after dinner, didn't you see her? She was only gone five minutes, wasn't she, John? She came back to try on her costume for the school play. Your Danny can't be out in this weather, surely?

– c'mon. I'll get my boots on. Get the big torch, will you, love? We'll have a look round the yard. He's a funny little chap, that one.

Their light flashes into the garage, into the stables, between the orchard trees, the corners of the coal bunker. They can hardly hear each other in the wind. In the porch Peter speaks rapidly.

– he must be back in the house after all. Patrick looked upstairs but – maybe he's got into the attic somehow. He won't come, when you call. He's a little scamp. He must be there. Thanks, John.

– come back if you've no luck. Devil of a night.

He's running. Back into the house, upstairs, along the passage. The trap door to the attic is shut; the ladder is not there. He can't climb the walls. Patrick, check the rooms again, cupboards, beds, curtains, everywhere. I'll check the shed with the torch, the hen house... oh God. The well.

He shines his torch on the pump, on the well head.

Nothing has changed since he covered it with the hen house door yesterday morning. The big stones on top are in exactly the same positions, yes, they are. They've held, even in this wind. He still has a liminal image of the boy down there, and tells himself to be rational. Nobody could be down the well and replace the lid with stones on top. Get a grip on yourself.

In the kitchen he opens his hands in a gesture of despair. Brenda looks at him with blank eyes.

– is there anyone else he could've gone to? Patrick?

– no. I can't think.

– the church? Does he ever go there?

– no.

– it's worth a look.

– shall I come?

– stay with your mother.

Peter shouts into the dark church and crawls on his hands and knees under the altar. He's shouting for Danny and for God but he's on the wrong track towards understanding either of them.

———

A house of worship would not attract Danny; he has never thought to enter one by himself. He is drawn, now that his legs are long enough to take him, over the fields and down towards the west. On mornings bunked off from school and afternoons when no one has looked for him, he has ventured further and further from the top of the island to the coast. Not to the sea but the nooks and crannies of the land, the dolmens on the headlands and the cottages where the fishermen sleep over their shifting sandy beds.

On the sides of old walls he watches the strange pale beetles move like fossil things, slipping into cracks to wait out another few ages of man. He'll not leave this place for anyone – Melissa has warned him about their plans. He'll dig himself into the cracks and then let's see if they can make him go.

The weather understands him. The wind yells between the stones like a yell he feels coming up inside. The sky is black and rushing and flying horses thunder over his head. He can step up into his chariot any time and gallop away.

———

At ten o'clock that night John and Peter talk about calling the police. But it's not the way of country people, Brenda is adamant, no police. They agree reluctantly that the child *is* one to run off; it's his nature. Some kids wouldn't dream of it, but that one... He'll turn up somewhere. Yes, of course. We'll wait until first light.

Go to bed, Peter tells his neighbours. What can you do? Melissa watches with wide blue eyes from the top of the stairs. Go to bed, Peter tells Brenda and Patrick. I'll stay awake, in case.

Perhaps he does sleep, on and off. He goes out several

times, flashing a light uselessly into the darkness. He fills the coal scuttle, he paces around the kitchen, lifting things, putting them back. He finds a pile of unpaid bills stuffed behind the clock. When a burst of rain hits the window he imagines small white limbs in the wet earth.

ten

Early morning brings John Corbin, coming down the drive with a Thermos of coffee. The Vauquiers are out in their car already, searching the lanes. Best not to tell too many folk yet. Don't panic. He looks at Peter's face and sees that his friend is beyond panic.

   – should I go to school today, Dad?

   – hm? Oh, it's you, Patrick. Sorry.

   – should I?

   – yes, I should say so. Do you think so? Yes.

As Patrick eats his cornflakes the green Ford swings into view. On the back seat there is a bundle huddled into the corner under a blanket. As his father reaches for him, Danny opens his eyes and lets out a long wail.

   – *no!*

   – come on, my boy.

   – no!

   – let's just get you inside. Holy Father, this child's half frozen.

They talk in low, urgent voices over his head while Danny sobs. John is despatched to phone for a doctor and returns with a message from Deborah; bring Danny over, if he wants. She's warming the spare room for him. It might be better to have him over there where there's a phone.

– look, he's asleep.

– knocked himself out, more like.

– poor little mite. Where on earth...?

– in the corner by Sebire's place. Wandering about like an elf. Said he spent the night at Bash's. Think he did?

– come on. I'll carry him.

– praise be.

– thank God you found him, Bob.

– aye, well. You can't get far away on an island, can you?

– you have any brandy, Peter? Looks like you could do with some.

———

Peter doesn't know how the man came to be known as Bash. It's lost in time like most of the old fellow's mental faculties. Even these, no one can exactly determine. Bob Vauquier says that his name is in the records as Abelard Ozanne.

Patrick has gone to school. Danny is tucked up in bed at the Corbins'; Brenda is having a bath. Peter crackles with fatigue, but he couldn't sleep. He puts some change into his pockets – there are a few calls to make from the phone box, and he'll go the long way, past Sebire's. The walk will clear his head.

The air, after the last night's storm, would clear anything. It smarts in his eyes and sears in his lungs. What a lather, this last three days. How good it would be to live a plain and dull life again. How deceptive they are, these old grey walls of drowsing farms.

It's not so far, if you know the back ways. He had imagined the boy staggering around half the night on his five-year-old legs, dropping from exhaustion. Dying of exposure, even. But sheltering at Bash's is a likely explanation.

It's a lovely island, sure enough. Look at the lily meadows, flooded now, with the water table so high. There's the stream running under the road where he and Elsa used to float sticks. Years ago. There's Gavey's bull, in the field. Always a bull in that field. Different animals, but there's always one there. Nice to see a bit of sun coming out for a change.

Peter rounds the corner. There it is, look at that. Only a bungalow; must have been a neat little place, once. Look at the green mould running down from the windows, and the guttering all off. The hedges nearly meet across the path.

There he is, Abelard Ozanne himself. Tottering along on the other side of the road. Where does he go to, nowadays? To whom does he speak? Peter moves towards him; clears his throat.

– morning!

– aye.

– Mr Ozanne, isn't it?

Abelard Ozanne fixes him with a rheumy stare. Different expressions flit across his face, but none of them settle. He doesn't seem in a hurry to acknowledge the name. Perhaps it isn't him, after all. Peter has only the vaguest idea, yet he feels sure that it is.

– lovely spot.

– aye.

– this your house?

– it wouldn't be.

– you're Mr Ozanne, aren't you?

Again the enigmatic look, the face working slowly, a rumination. The salivary mouth puckers in and out but delivers no reply. Peter tries another approach.

– d'you know who lives here?

– eh?

– you know who lives here?

The old man regards the house as though he has never seen it before.

– folks ask that. Ah don't know.

– nice spot.

– ah. Would be.

– there was a young lad around here last night, was there?

Silence, and more saliva.

– all right, then. Bye, Mr Ozanne.

– goodbye to ye.

———

– Susan?

– Peter?

– I'm in a phone box again. Not so far away this time, though. You all right?

– yes, fine. I heard you were over.

– oh? Who said?

– my mum.

– all the details, too?

– she said you arrived Friday, at the airport. One of her spies probably saw you.

Peter crinkles up his face into a smile.

– reckon we could dodge them long enough to have tea together? Would you like to?

– we could try.

– when are you free?

– do you want to make it at the weekend, and bring the boys?

– I thought we might go in the week, while they're still at school. Do you have a free morning?

– Thursday?

– Thursday's fine. Where?

– in town?

– spies everywhere. I know just the place.

eleven

Christmas with all those people being nice to her would be more than she could stand. All that carolling going on in the church. Brenda packs her bags. Not that anything fits her any more; she doesn't look when she passes the mirror. He's engulfed her, distorted her. The rage is as fresh as ever, but now it is further down. This *thing* is the cause of it. He'll know about it, you may be sure. He'd have come back for her, otherwise.

Another two months; it seems like forever.

– I'm ready.

– come on, then.

It seems all wrong to Peter, taking her by bus. Taking his pregnant wife away by bus from her home and children. How could he tell Patrick: when you come home from school your mum is going to be gone. But how else? Take the boy with them on the bus? Danny, at least, is still living with the Corbins. The doctor says there's no danger, no physical harm done, but the lad seems fixed to his bed.

They stand under the dripping elms, waiting for the number eleven. Hoping that nobody will come by. At least it's mid morning, and Mrs Pickery won't be on the bus. Her eyes would pop clean out of her head.

They'll go to the adoption agency now, after they've dropped off Brenda's things. That is their agreement. He'll take her back to the flat, and she'll keep the appointment.

He looks down at the ends of his shoes. He feels that he is the one to blame for her fate, though he is not sure how or why. Even if she changed her mind now, it wouldn't do any good, and he hasn't asked her to.

They are not unseen. The bus stop is just visible from the upstairs window at the Corbins'.

———

Susan Pickery parks outside the Cross Keys Café on Thursday morning and glances up into the mirror. She's got an anxious look on her face. He made it sound like fun on the phone, but now it seems a fraction underhand. Oh, but there's no harm – it's only a cup of tea. Her mother knows nothing about it, Susan is reasonably sure.

There's his bicycle up against the hedge. She hangs back, fiddling with her keys.

Peter sits at a table, from where he can see the door, though not the car park. He felt fine about this on Monday; it had seemed to be an ordinary, nice idea. He'd been overwrought that morning. He should never have suggested this café. He's just going around in circles. The woman behind the counter looks as if she remembers him.

Brenda was so dazzling on that day when they met here, and sort of *terrible*. She sat right *there*. He left her in town just yesterday, after all those questions they had asked – about whether they live as husband and wife and everything. She, stony-faced through it all. Now here he is, carrying on, the very next day. Not carrying on exactly; it's only a cup of tea.

– hello.

– hello.

– you've grown a beard.

– ah! Yes.

– you look different.

– you look… the same.

They smile. She does look the same. A little more solid, maybe; just a touch. She smells of soap.

– shall I order?

– just tea, please.

He goes to the counter, looking the woman very straight in the eye as he orders tea for two. He remembers Hilda Pickery's spies, and laughs to himself.

– shall I pour?

– please.

– do you still take sugar?

– just the one, thank you.

– how's Danny?

– you heard? I suppose you did. He's up out of bed

now, since yesterday. Patrick and I went over but he wouldn't *look* at us, not really. I told him that we might go away for Christmas and he started wailing again – I've never heard anything like it. I thought it might brighten him up a bit.

   – going for Christmas?

   – that's the idea. We've plenty of cousins over there, and second cousins – boys of the same age. They've planned a family reunion over the New Year.

   – a new beginning, in a way?

   – well, just to see how it goes, yes.

   – oh.

———

At this very moment, Susan's father is issuing out for his morning walk. The Swan will be opening shortly. He cranes back his head and then nods to himself with satisfaction. He knew it. Them curtains have moved. He knew he'd heard something yesterday from next door and Hilda said how could he hear anything, what with him being so deaf. That one's back, then. Now we'll see if what they say is true...

Brenda waits until his brown cap has vanished around the corner and then puts on her coat. Good job she kept this old thing. The buttons still meet, and she can move them an inch or so; it'll probably last right through. It's only round the middle she is showing, the rest of her isn't any bigger. Thinner, if anything. Her ankles are trim; she'll pass. If it were summer – well, that would be another story.

She takes up her bag and her purse and leaves the flat. She'll pop in to Jackie at the shoe shop and that'll get the ball rolling. The boys'll know by tonight that she's back – the bars in town carry the news as efficiently as the church in the country. She could do with having a laugh again. She'll get in a bottle or two, when she goes on to Chandra's. Look at all those lights down by the square. She feels better already.

———

Susan stirs her tea. Mortified, she knows that her disappointment must be written all over her face. He hasn't come back for good, he's just fetching his children.

– Susan?

– yes?

– thought you were dreaming for a minute. I wanted to say – well, sorry, like, for asking you to come over that time. It was wrong of me.

– no! Oh no.

So he even wishes he'd never asked her. What a fool she was; she lost her chance, sure enough.

– it wasn't fair of me, I realised afterwards. I couldn't expect you to drop everything, could I? And what would people have thought?

– I didn't look at it like that. It wasn't that...

– ... it's a mistake I make when I get worried – I panic

and I don't think things through. So that's why I want to ask now, while I'm here – not in a phone box for once...

    – ask?

    – ... if you'd come over? If we stayed there, that is. I mean come for a proper holiday when you've got the time. Think about it.

twelve

Every soul pulls with the tide and hears, on some level, the waves that break out there in the dark. In The Navigator, Brenda is having a quick half with Willy le Cras. She'll walk him home in a while, or maybe it will be the other way around. He gazes mistily into the phantasmagoric world between the optics. Brenda winks at Henry. There's a temporary girl behind the bar; her job is kept for her, when she's ready.

A little further on from the bar in which they sit, the road turns into a leafy street of fine residential homes. Brenda and Willy will pass the end of this street in about twenty minutes and never give it a thought. In a tall white house there's a fire-lit sitting room where Dr de Garis sits with his wife, hand in hand on the sofa. He has poured a sherry for them both with which to celebrate the news. They've been on the waiting list for so long; the nursery upstairs has been prepared for so many months, and now – at last.

———

Peter draws the curtains closed. Friday evening. The house feels different with just the two of them, Patrick and himself. He's never known just two in the house before. Last night he slept, as he will tonight, where his wife had been sleeping before him. He allows himself this last and unexpected pleasure, hugging the sheets and pillows to his face while his rational mind reverses along the tracks of his love.

He opens the flue in the Aga a notch. Patrick lifts his head for a moment and grins over his book. They've done a lot today. It was good to be up on the roof, showing the boy how to handle the slates. The hen house is swept out; the wire all cleaned and rolled up. The drains are done. He's cancelled the phone repairs; no point in that.

There's a knock at the door.

– I'll get it.

– good lad.

– Dad, it's Mr Corbin.

– evening, John. Come and sit yourself down.

– evening.

– can I get you something?

– no, no. I just wanted a word.

– shall you go for your bath, Patrick?

– hm? Oh, okay.

– how's Danny? Time he came home, now.

– he's well enough. That's what I want to talk about.

Deborah agreed with me. Her idea, in fact. You're expecting to take the boys away next week, isn't it. Young Danny isn't keen on the idea.

– I know.

– but you can't wait around – the flights will be full. Fact is, the boy wants to stay with us, and we're willing. If you are.

Peter shifts in his chair.

– not that we want to push ourselves in where it's not our business – but it could be like a holiday for the lad, at our place.

– has he said anything?

– not in plain words, but in his own way.

– I was wondering how to persuade him away, to be honest. If he truly seems... you can manage the extra one for Christmas?

– you know we can.

– he's a handful, sometimes.

– we know.

– ah, you should! I'll pay his keep...

– we can arrange something.

– but I feel like, like I'll be leaving him again. Seems the last thing he needs.

– he's determined to get himself left, more like.

———

The flights are booked, the bills are paid. Over the lid of the well Peter pours a thin layer of cement. Easy enough to break when John needs water for his cows, but safe in any weather from inquisitive children.

He leaves the house ready for his sister. There are logs in the woodpile, the floors are swept, the spare key lodged under the brick. Each practical thought is a leave-taking.

It is Patrick's first ride all the way into town by bicycle, on a crisp December morning with his father. The world spreads out and gets bigger. He can compass the miles with his wheels, conquer the island and step off from there, further and further. Peter pedals slowly, watching the boy ahead of him, mindful of the traffic. He left a message at the bakery for Brenda, telling her that they were coming. They can hardly exchange Christmas presents, can they? But at least they can say goodbye.

At the door of Number 5, they stand and wait. They knock, and stand and wait. Just a minute, says Peter. He crosses to the bakery where they assure him that yes, they gave her the message; they spoke to her personally. He knocks once more. Through the net curtains, the Pickerys watch.

Peter takes the Christmas card out of his pocket and seals it because of the fifty pounds inside and pushes it through the letter box. He puts an arm over his son's shoulder and pulls him gently away.

thirteen

She doesn't want to know, and they have agreed to her wishes. She doesn't know that it's a baby girl wrapped up in a towel and taken from the room. She sleeps.

The infant is weighed and checked and the Nursing Home later dials the number of the de Garis house. In her dressing gown Helen de Garis lifts the telephone receiver. It's a girl, it's a girl, she tells her husband. They embrace. They've already chosen names for the child they are adopting, and the name they have chosen for a girl is Sarah.